A Catoctin Christmas

A Sweet Holiday
Friends to Lovers Romance

CHAS WILLIAMSON

Print ISBN: 978-1-64649-521-4

eBook ISBN: 978-1-64649-522-1

 Year of the Book
135 Glen Avenue
Glen Rock, PA 17327

Prelude

*M*egan McKenzie opened the door of the office in the Temple district of London. The building was old and the scent of the air freshener didn't quite mask the musty smell of old papers that seemed to emanate from all corners of the office.

"May I help you?" asked a middle-aged woman with horned-rimmed glasses.

"Hi, uh, I'm here to see Mr. Chamberlain."

"Which one?" the woman asked smartly as she batted her eyelids. "George the second, third or fourth?"

"I'll handle this, Hattie," came a deep voice from a back room. A man Megan knew well from his frequent associations with her grandmother stepped next to the receptionist's desk.

"Afternoon, sir," Megan said as she acknowledged George Chamberlain the second.

The man offered his hand. "I'd like to offer my condolences once again at your grandmother's passing."

"Thank you." He had been at the funeral and was one of the few in attendance who actually shed real tears.

"I believe my grandson handled her will. Let me walk you to his office." The man led the way up richly carpeted stairs to a spacious oak-paneled second floor with twelve-foot ceilings. Bookshelves in the open area housed hundreds, if not thousands, of what appeared to be legal manuals.

A middle-aged version of George the second popped out of the center office. "You must be Ms. McKenzie. I'm George Chamberlain the third. I've heard quite a bit about you and am honored to make your acquaintance."

"It's nice to meet you as well, sir," Megan replied with a slight nod of her head. She neither liked nor trusted anyone named Chamberlain, starting with the youngest and extending to the eldest. Why her grandmother chose this firm to represent her was beyond Megan's understanding.

A young man appeared from the corner room. Megan had been exposed to him all her life. It was the same man her grandmother desperately wanted Megan to marry, but if there was one thing Megan couldn't stand, it was this dunce.

As soon as his eyes met Megan's, a suggestive smile covered his face. The slant to his expression creeped her out. A shiver began at the base of her spine that ran up and across her shoulders.

"Nice to see you again, Meg. You look lovely today."

She didn't appreciate the way George Chamberlain the fourth acted as if they were close friends. That most certainly never was the case and certainly never would be.

"In the future, you may refer to me as Megan, thank you." From the corner of her eye, she took note of the expression that the young man's father and grandfather shared. "I believe I'm here to review my grandmother's will."

"That you are," replied the youngest man with a wink. "Come on into my office and, uh, let's get comfortable, shall we?" His eyes roved over Megan's body, but failed to reach her eyes. An unpleasant taste rose in her throat.

The eldest of the three briefly stared at Megan. "Would you mind if I sat in on the reading of the will?" The expression of displeasure on the youngest man's face was quite apparent.

Thank God! "That would be appreciated, since you were a close friend of my grandmother." Megan suspected the man had been more than a friend, but she decided not to think ill of those who had passed on.

Once inside the office of George the fourth, the younger man removed a file from a safe behind his desk. Megan took the chair farthest from him. He handed Megan a sheaf of printed papers. Young George opened his mouth to speak but was interrupted.

"Before you read the will, grandson, let me explain a few things to Megan." The old man turned to her. "It's no secret your grandmother was once engaged to me, before your grandfather won her heart. God rest his soul, but the poor man died right after your mother was born."

"My grandmother told me more than once how you helped her over the years." *Help? Yeah right—*

despite the fact you were married to another woman.

"I did. I advised her on how best to invest your grandfather's meager insurance proceeds."

Must not have been very good advice. I wore second-hand clothes all my life and we lived off the generosity of others. "Thank you."

He partially closed one eye as he looked at her. "I'm not sure if she ever shared with you what the returns were on that investment."

"We lived within our means."

"No, you most certainly did not," he replied with a laugh.

"I beg your pardon?" Megan certainly didn't appreciate his tone or how he was making fun of her.

"Megan, that meager investment of a thousand pounds grew, astronomically."

"I'm not following you."

"Do you know your grandmother's net worth?"

"Uh, no."

"A little over five and a half million pounds."

"What?" Her whole body shook uncontrollably. "Either I didn't hear you correctly or there must be some mistake. We lived like paupers and stood in line at soup kitchens weekly."

"Because that was the way your grandmother chose to live. Do you know what she was saving her money for?"

"No."

"You, my dear."

"Excuse me?"

"Your grandmother continually reinvested her wealth so you could have a rich and happy life—one much different than her self-imposed frugality."

The room was beginning to spin and Megan's lunch didn't seem to sit very well in her stomach. She grabbed onto the desk to steady herself. "Are you telling me after all these years of being poor, now I'm rich?"

"There are just a few requirements you must meet before you can access the trust," interrupted George the fourth.

"There are?" questioned his grandfather. "Such as?"

When the young man read that portion of the will, Megan's dizziness became worse and suddenly darkness overtook her. The last thing Megan remembered before the floor rushed up to meet her was George the second's outburst.

"That's preposterous! Show me the proof."

Megan wasn't conscious to hear the answer.

Chapter One

The sudden shudder of the aircraft aroused Megan from her slumber. The overhead speaker came to life. "The captain has turned on the seat belt sign. We've run into a bit of turbulence but should soon be past it. All passengers must return to their seats and fasten their seat belts."

She glanced out of the window. There was now land below them instead of the blue of the Atlantic. Megan's heart skipped a beat. "My first glimpse of America, the land of my hope." The plane continued to descend and after a while, Megan noted the blur of green disappear as the airliner flew above another body of water. "That would be the Chesapeake." Although she had yet to set foot in the United States, Megan felt she knew this country well. *Okay, as thoroughly as one might from reading a book and looking at maps.*

The speaker again crackled to life. "Ladies and gentlemen, we are making our final approach to the Baltimore-Washington's Thurgood Marshall International Airport. Please return your seats and tray tables to the upright position. Currently, the temperature on the ground is eighty-seven degrees and the skies are clear, with a visibility of seventeen miles. On behalf of this Atlanta-based flight crew, welcome to Baltimore." Megan's mind was buzzing and the rest of the overhead messages about connecting flights were blurred out.

It had been eight years since she'd last seen Taylor Davis, back when her friend was an exchange teacher at Megan's school in London. Despite a ten-year age difference, the two had become steadfast friends. Their friendship had continued through the years, despite not seeing each other face to face. It was Taylor, in fact, who had encouraged Megan to apply as an exchange teacher in the same district where Taylor taught.

The plane landed smoothly and after a brief delay getting through Customs, Megan struggled with her luggage. She finally arrived at the receiving area. Scanning the crowd, she noted a man holding a sign with her name on it. Despite his attire not being what she expected for a gentleman, there was a certain something about him that piqued her interest. He wore dungarees and a T-shirt with an emblem that looked like a deer on a telly screen. His resemblance to Taylor was obvious. Megan surmised the man hadn't shaved in days. He sported a white, orange and black ball cap with the smiling face of some ridiculous bird. She approached him.

"Excuse me, I'm Megan. Are you looking for me?"

"No," the man replied with a frown, "but she is." He pointed to his left and a lady emerged from the crush.

"Megan! Welcome to America." Although Taylor appeared to have aged a bit, Megan recognized her immediately. "I'm so glad you're here." After hugs, her friend handed her a paper cup. "This is a café mocha, your favorite American drink, if I recall."

"Thank you. You remembered well. Somewhere in my carryon, I have some Earl Grey and a loaf of seeded cake tucked away."

"Here, I'll take your bags." The man handed Taylor the sign and hoisted all three of Megan's suitcases as if they weighed nothing. His voice was gruff. "Let's catch the bus to the parking area out here and get away from these crowds." The dirty work boots he wore must have been jet-propelled because he quickly led the way through sliding doors to the curbside.

"I assume he's your brother, but what's his problem?"

Megan's whispered question must have amused Taylor because her friend laughed.

"That's my brother, Brendon. He's not all that bad once you get to know him."

"He seems annoyed. Is that because of me?"

"No. He's got a lot going on at the farm. Summer is his busy season, but he readily volunteered to drive today. He knows how much I dislike the interstate and driving in big cities. He and I look out for each other."

Okay, maybe he and I got off on the wrong foot. "Is he what you Americans call a red face?"

Taylor stopped, turned to Megan and shot her a confused expression. "Red face? Oh my, I think you mean redneck." Taylor shook her head and threaded her arm through Megan's. "No, my brother is simply a good old boy."

"I can see I've got a lot to learn about America and the frailties of your version of the English language."

"Then let's begin your lessons."

Taylor led Megan out to where the man stood. She again took in his muscular build and her face turned warm when he glanced in her direction. Despite the irritated expression, he was cute.

"I'm looking forward to it."

***

"Are you sure you don't want to come to church with me?"

Brendon turned to see his sister's face. Although he firmly believed in God, he rarely set foot in church. That was because he suspected Trina Lewis would be there—ready to turn his world upside down and break his heart—yet again.

"I'll pass, but why don't you take your friend?"

"It's been a long day for Megan. Between the flight, our lunch down at Inner Harbor, and the time difference, she told me she'd like to turn in early."

"Great. I was afraid you would ask me to keep her entertained."

Taylor laughed and Brendon noted the twinkle in her eye. His little sister had been trying to play matchmaker for him for a while now. He had always come up with an excuse. After the way Trina betrayed him, Brendon had grown wary of women. And he certainly wasn't going to make an exception for the British girl who was staying with them.

"I was wondering..."

"Don't go there. You know the answer."

She raised her eyebrows. "May I finish?"

"Sure."

"Can you show her around the place while I'm gone?"

Perfect. That will delay getting my chores done. Brendon was hoping to finish early because the Ravens were hosting the San Diego Chargers in Baltimore's last pre-season game.

"Do I have to?"

"Have to what?"

Both siblings looked in the direction of the staircase, where the young Brit stood. Megan had changed clothes. She now sported jean shorts, sandals and a shirt with the image of four men in a crosswalk. He'd seen that picture before, but didn't know exactly where. However, what really caught his eye was the smile on her face.

Taylor responded. "I asked Bren if he would mind giving you a tour of the farm."

The girl's smile disappeared. "I see. That's fine, however, I wouldn't wish to impose on your brother's hospitality."

Why is it I always come off as the bad guy? "I, uh, didn't mean it like it sounded."

"Then how did you mean it?" Megan's stare unnerved him a bit.

"I just have chores to finish."

The Brit's right eye raised and he knew she expected him to elaborate.

"I need to feed the cows, collect the eggs from the henhouse and feed Orville—my dog—the one you met earlier."

"I like animals. Might I tag along?"

"Uh, sure, but you'll need different shoes."

"Here," Taylor said as she motioned for Megan to follow her. "You can use my work boots. I'll show you where they're at on my way out."

Normally Brendon would walk around the farm, but the pale girl seemed frail to him. While Megan was getting shoes from Taylor, he ran to the equipment shed.

His German Shepherd, Orville, jumped from the pet mattress on the porch and padded alongside. The dog hopped in the bed of the Gator, a four-wheel-drive farm utility vehicle. Brendon drove it to the porch. Megan was standing on the steps, waving goodbye as Taylor's Bronco headed down the lane.

"Hop on in."

The young woman approached but stopped short. She pointed to the side of the vehicle.

"That's the same emblem as the one on your shirt, isn't it?"

"Yep, That's the John Deere logo."

"I wondered what it represented."

"Now you know. What's with the four guys on your shirt?"

She glanced down and then stared at him in apparent disbelief. "Seriously?"

"Like, yeah. Who are they?"

"It's the Beatles, from the Abbey Road album. You don't know who they are?"

"I don't get out much, so sorry about that."

There was a silence between them as he drove to the feed lot. He parked the Gator and climbed out. "I'll only be ten minutes or so."

He manipulated the controls at a silo so he could transfer feed for the cattle to the various troughs in the open-air barn. As Brendon turned, he found Megan standing next to him.

"I don't think I've ever seen so many cows in one place."

"I've got about two-hundred head in this herd."

"What are their names?"

"Names?" He couldn't help but laugh. "Why would we name them?"

"Well, aren't they your pets?"

"This is a working farm. I bring them in as calves, feed them until they weigh between 800 and 1000 pounds and then sell them for..."

She held her hands in front of her. "Please, don't tell me." Megan looked a little queasy.

"This is my business, how I make an income."

"I see," she whispered before turning around and returning to the Gator.

He felt bad and didn't quite know what to say. "I didn't know you were a vegetarian."

"I'm not. I just didn't realize... you know?"

He backed the Gator up. Glancing across the seat, he noted Orville's head on the girl's lap. She was staring at the horizon while she petted the dog's ears.

"Sorry, Megan. I didn't mean to offend you."

"It's okay. You can call me Meg, if you would like."

He chanced another look in her direction and caught a smile.

"I would like that."

The remainder of his chores were pleasant. Megan had never collected eggs before. While the hens were fenced in to protect them from predators, they were free-range.

Brendon showed Megan the favorite places where the hens would lay. They ended up with a large basket of brown eggs.

Finally, they returned to the porch. The young lady sat on the top step and wiped her brow. Her blue eyes seemed to sparkle as she took him in.

"I bet you're exhausted."

"That I am. Think I'll hit the shower and then call it a night. Thanks for the tour."

"My pleasure. Perhaps we can do it again sometime?"

"Why? You weren't excited for me to tag along."

His face began to warm. "Maybe not at first, but it turned out to be kind of fun. No pressure, but if you'd like to go again, just say the word."

She hesitated before replying. Her eyes seemed to be assessing him. Finally, she answered. "We'll see. Good night."

"You, too."

With a slight nod, Megan disappeared behind the screen door. Brendon plopped down on the stairs and brushed the dirt from his pants. Orville dropped down next to him and then rolled on his back so Brendon could scratch his tummy.

But his thoughts weren't on his dog. They were on the girl he'd spent the last two hours with doing chores. His heartbeat was stronger than he remembered. *Is that because of her?*

Closing his eyes, Megan's face materialized before him. But then another image replaced it—Trina's.

Shaking his head, Brendon stood. "I need to stop this before it starts. I am *not* going to allow my heart to be broken again."

Chapter Two

Megan turned off the alarm and stared at the digital display. It read five-thirty, which was a half hour earlier than she normally got out of bed. But today was different. Taylor and her boyfriend were going away for a three-day weekend. Megan wished to see her friend off.

The enticing scent of coffee greeted Megan as she walked down the stairs.

Garbled voices slipped out from under the kitchen door. Megan was curious about the conversation.

"Be kind to her while I'm away this weekend."

"I'm always nice."

"Really? You've avoided her for the entire time she's been here—all five weeks."

"Come on. You know this is my busy season. I was baling hay, fixing fences, getting the equipment ready for harvest... you know, things like that."

It probably wasn't the wisest thing to do, but Megan edged nearer to the closed door so she could eavesdrop on Taylor and Brendon's discussion more easily.

"No, brother. You've made sure you leave the house before she gets up and you've kept yourself busy until she turns in at night. And I'm positive you aren't working all day long. It's almost as if you are shunning Megan. Why? She's the nicest girl I know and a good friend. She's only here until Christmas. Do you want her to think all American guys are as stuck up as you?"

"Taylor, butt out of my business."

"I will, as soon as you tell me what's going on."

The volume of their voices dropped to whisper level. Megan tiptoed closer, but still wasn't able to hear. She was just about to ease the door open when a rumbling noise from outside startled her.

"Sounds like Chuck is here." Brendon's voice had returned to a conversational level.

"Invite him inside while I finish making coffee."

Megan quickly retreated back to the stairs and posed as if she had just reached the bottom tread.

The door flew open and Brendon walked through. His eyes were wide open when he addressed her. "Oh, uh, morning. How long were you standing there?"

"I just came down," she lied. "I wanted to see Taylor off."

"Okay, um, I'm going to invite her boyfriend inside."

"That's fine." Megan wasn't sure if it was her imagination, but Brendon's hands seemed shaky.

The man walked outside and returned with Chuck. Taylor's boyfriend had always been kind to Megan and acted the same this morning.

After a rapid flurry of activity, Megan found herself outside, next to Brendon, waving goodbye to the pair.

After the vehicle's lights disappeared, Megan cast a glance eastward toward the Catoctin Mountains. The sunrise wouldn't occur for another half hour. She felt Brendon's presence, but he didn't say anything. She wasn't sure why, but Taylor's brother seemed to dislike her.

"I'm going to get ready. Taylor made arrangements for one of the other teachers to stop by and fetch me for school."

She had turned and was three treads up before he spoke.

"Megan? I mean, Meg? I don't mind taking you. In fact, while you get ready, I'll pour you a cup of coffee and make your breakfast." Megan was about to tell him no thanks when he continued. "I believe you like café mocha and normally eat two soft-boiled eggs. Am I right?"

She felt her mouth drop open. "How do you know that? You've never stayed for breakfast with us."

"True," the man answered as he stepped closer. "But usually I am the one who puts the dirty dishes in the dishwasher."

"That may explain the eggs, but what about the coffee. What, do you sniff the cup?"

Brendon burst out laughing. It was so contagious that Megan joined in. "Do you think I'm some pervert?"

"Either that or you're clairvoyant."

The man shook his head. "No, there's a much simpler explanation. I also empty the garbage. Since

Taylor drinks tea and I prefer Hawaiian coffee, that means the mocha pods are most likely yours."

"Wow, Sherlock, I'm impressed. I guess maybe it does."

"Seriously, I wouldn't mind driving you to school, if... if that's okay with you."

The butterflies she'd felt the day she met Brendon suddenly migrated back to her stomach.

"I guess that would be fine. Perhaps I could cancel my ride."

"Please do. I'll start your eggs."

Megan watched as he returned to the enclosed kitchen. Her mind replayed her time in America. Taylor had made the effort to introduce Megan to this country each weekend. Together they had explored Washington, New York, Boston, and Philadelphia. With her friend on a jaunt with her beau, Megan expected a lonely solitary weekend, but now?

"Hmm, perhaps this weekend won't be as boring as I dreaded."

***

Brendon slid the pickup into a space outside the elementary school and waited. His body trembled as he anticipated Megan's arrival. After the discussion he'd had with Taylor earlier in the day, he had discovered Megan on the stairs. Thank goodness she hadn't heard the conversation he and Taylor had shared.

"Taylor, butt out of my business."

"I will, as soon as you tell me what's going on."

He had lowered his voice. "I don't know what you are talking about."

"Look, you might be able to hide your feelings from my British friend, but I know you too well. Spill your thoughts. You act as if you don't like her, but that isn't entirely correct. Am I right?"

Brendon hesitated before replying. "Okay. Megan is cute and polite."

"That she is, and let me guess... you care for her."

"I didn't say that."

"Not in so many words, but be honest with me. Are you attracted to her?"

"I could easily see that happening, except for one thing."

Taylor's expression softened. "Trina?"

"I'm scared to allow myself to ever care for someone. That's why I never date... or even talk to Megan."

"That witch really did a number on you. You do realize Trina was the exception, not the rule when it comes to how women treat men."

"Maybe, but—"

The sound of tires on gravel interrupted them.

"Hello, sir. Come here often?"

Brendon jumped at the voice. His pulse slowed when he found Megan standing outside his car door.

He quickly jumped out and took her book bag. It only took a few seconds to realize she had dressed in older clothes and sneakers, just as Brendon had suggested before he took her to school. Not that it mattered... her smile could light up any room.

"I haven't been here in years. I only came to pick you up." He opened the passenger door and offered his hand.

She climbed inside, looked him square in the face and shook her head. "You're either forgetful or a liar," Megan giggled when he started the truck.

"What?"

"How quickly you forget you dropped me off, just this morning. Or maybe you don't remember because I'm not important to you."

The warmth of her teasing smile took all his cares away. "In my defense, it is hard to concentrate when I'm in the presence of such a charming lady." He noted a slight blush on her cheeks. *Are we actually flirting with each other?*

Megan cleared her throat. "Anyway, you told me we were going to visit somewhere special tonight. Would you like to share?"

"Of course. I packed a picnic supper we can eat after we hike up to the falls at Cunningham State Park." He pointed to an insulated bag on the floor. "I grabbed some water and a snack in case you were hungry or thirsty before our walk."

She didn't reply and he glanced at her. "Wow. I didn't expect this. Maybe you are as nice as Taylor claims."

"I guess that remains to be seen. Now, might I make a request, my lady?"

"Perhaps."

"Tell me about your day and who Megan McKenzie really is. At least one inquiring mind wants to know."

Chapter Three

*T*he sun was dipping low on the western horizon. The joy of the day, coupled with soft country music and perfectly set air-conditioning had Megan on the verge of slumber. She knew memories of the sights they had seen on the Skyline Drive would stay in her heart forever.

"I hope our trip today didn't bore you too much." Brendon's words interrupted her desire to nap.

"Of course not. Why would you say that?"

"I know Taylor has taken you to the big cities, where there are museums, shopping and all kinds of sightseeing opportunities. Today had to be a let-down, riding on backroads and stopping at mountain overlooks. You probably think I'm a hick."

"I thoroughly enjoyed the sights and you taking me. Wait, your words confuse me. Is a hick the same thing as a red-face or is it similar to a country boy?"

Brendon burst out in laughter. "What in the world is a red-face?"

"I'm sorry," she giggled. "Taylor already corrected me once. I meant to say redneck. Is that the same thing as a hick?"

Glancing at the man who was driving, her heart warmed. His face displayed that gentle smile again, which she was beginning to learn suggested he was about to tease her.

"I think the pecking order goes like this: a country boy is top shelf, a hick is mid-level and a redneck is like the bottom of the barrel."

"I see." If the man could tease her, well, he should be able to take it. "Which classification do you fall into?"

"Well, if you have to ask, I suspect the country boy category is out." He turned in her direction and smiled. "I guess being a hick isn't that bad. Of course, when I was in the Army, everyone called me a redneck."

"Oh, I hadn't realized you served your country."

"My plans on becoming a high school English teacher fizzled out. I joined the service, planning to make a career out of it until Dad's health turned bad. I gave it up so we could continue the family farm."

"So sorry to hear that. Is he okay now?"

"His cancer has been in remission for years. He and Mom live in Arizona." Brendon's brow furrowed. "I'm surprised Taylor didn't tell you about Mom and Dad... or me, for that matter."

"She did, but I wanted to hear your version of the story. You see, Taylor is my best friend and we have no secrets." *Well, that's a great big fat lie.*

"What?" he squawked in apparent surprise. "Were you trying to verify if what Taylor said was true or see if I would lie to you?"

"Neither. I simply wanted to hear what you thought."

"Did I do okay?"

He was acting a bit miffed, but Megan was pretty sure she could see right through him. "There was no right or wrong answer. I wanted to understand how you put things."

"Hold on a second."

Megan noted a change in his expression to possibly one of fear.

"What exactly *did* Taylor tell you about me?"

"Let's see. She told me you're a farmer who is totally devoted to his family. She hinted you're a bit of a loner. On the other hand, Taylor did say you can clean up well, if you try very, very hard." Megan enjoyed the way his eyes lit up.

"My little sister said what?"

"That's not important right now." Megan stopped to take in his profile. She waited until he glanced in her direction. "Taylor also told me you are one of the good ones—a man who knows right from wrong and that your heart is usually in the right place."

"Humph. That's a little better, I guess."

"Would you like to know what I think about you?"

Brendon's cheeks turned bright pink. "Uh, no. Not yet." His response surprised her.

"May I ask why not?"

"Because I haven't allowed you to see the real me."

"We spent yesterday afternoon and all day today together. If that wasn't you, who was it? Brad Pitt?"

"I wasn't talking about recently. I did you a disservice by kind of ignoring you since you got here."

Megan reached across the truck seat and touched his arm. "I noticed that. Why did you act that way?"

"Something happened in my past."

"Would you like to talk about it?"

"No. I mean, not right now. Maybe someday I'll share what went down. You know, today has been fun and I don't want to put a damper on it. Can we change the subject?" Once again, he directed his attention right at Megan. "Please?"

"As you wish. Would you like to talk about something else, or perhaps you'd prefer driving in silence?"

He paused in his response and Megan noted a redness start to rise up his neck. "I kind of like the sound of your voice, you know, with the accent and all. Maybe I could find out more about you?"

"Okay, what would you like to know?"

"Well, you and Taylor are friends, but why in all the universe would you want to come to the States, especially to rural Maryland?"

"I don't know. I've always been intrigued with your country. When I was younger, I used to compare the size of Great Britain to America. Did you know your country is almost four thousand times larger than mine?"

"I guess I didn't realize that."

Megan pushed her bangs from her eyes. "Considering that there are only five times as many of you Yanks compared to us Brits, that means there is a lot of open space. And when I read about the wonders of your country, I couldn't help but fall in love with it. You don't know how lucky you are to live here."

"I'll have to disagree with you on that. I did two tours in Afghanistan and that made me not only realize my good fortune, but it reminded me to thank God every day that I am living in the land of the free."

"I'm glad you understand your blessing of being born here. I'd give my right arm to be an American."

The truck swerved slightly and Megan realized it was because Brendon had again looked in her direction. "Don't you miss London?"

"A little, but there's not much for me to return to. I have no family. My mother died when I was young."

"I'm so sorry to hear that. What about your father?"

"I never knew him. My grandmother raised me. She passed last spring."

"My heart goes out to you for your loss. Certainly you had a boyfriend, didn't you?"

Megan had to be careful here. She hadn't even revealed the truth to Taylor. "Between my looks and being a very private person, I don't think I've had more than five dates in my life. My grandmother taught me to be cautious—of everything and everyone. Always tried to protect me, but I suspect I'll die an elderly spinster." *If I'm lucky.*

"Your looks? What do you think is wrong with your appearance?"

Megan's eyebrows raised. "Did you not notice the plethora of freckles on my face—or how plain I appear? I'm certainly not as attractive as most girls."

"Your freckles are cute—like beauty marks. And you're being hard on yourself. I rather think of you as the girl next door."

"What is that supposed to mean?"

"To me, that means a clean, wholesome type of female who is kind, sweet and down to earth—the kind most men would want to spend their life with. I personally think way too much emphasis is placed on a girl's supposed 'beauty and figure'. You know, those things fade away in time, but in my mind, the kindness a woman possesses in her heart is what's not only important, but the most attractive attribute a lady has."

"Taylor did say you weren't like most men," Megan muttered.

"Excuse me?"

"Uh, nothing. Mind if we change the subject?"

She noted he drew a long breath before speaking. "Why don't you want to go home?"

"There's not much waiting there for me. I just feel like this year will be the zenith of my life. Going back to London means accepting a life of less—like falling asleep after a great dream. I don't have a sibling like Taylor waiting for me."

Megan turned to watch the landscape slip by. It was hard to believe she'd just shared some of her deepest thoughts and fears with Taylor's brother. *What's wrong with me?* She'd let her guard down and her grandmother would have scolded her. *At least I didn't tell Brendon about... him.*

The warmth of Brendon's touch on her arm shocked her. She pivoted to look at him.

"I want to say this *and* I want you to really listen."

"Okay?" Her body suddenly tingled with anticipation.

"You do have a family—and that's Taylor and me. It makes me sad, hearing your mindset about returning home. Maybe it's time to look for a new one... here in America. Would you consider that?"

"But I'm only here on a visa for five months. How could I possibly stay?"

"Well, that's something we'll have to figure out, together—as in you, Taylor and me. I think it would be great if you stayed here."

A glance at his face revealed something she hadn't seen before, but what was it?

"Remaining here would be nice, but let's be realistic. Right after Christmas, I'm returning to Merry Old England." She lowered her voice. "No matter how desperately I'd rather not go."

"There's only one thing to do."

"Meaning?"

"We'll come up with a plan. I mean, after all, you're here in the land of the free, a country where anything is possible."

"Wait! By the look on your face, do you already have a plan?"

"Not yet. I think we should ask God's help on this. Is that okay?"

"I guess."

"Good evening, Father. We thank You for the beauty of the world around us. Your daughter, Megan, likes it here in America. Please help us work out a plan so she can stay here. And help my new friend find peace, contentment and joy in her life. Amen."

"Amen. That was sweet. Thank you."

Perhaps God really would assist her in getting out of the dilemma she was in. Thoughts of the possibility of a real future warmed her spirit.

Withdrawing into her own thoughts, Psalm 37, verse 4, filled her heart. *'Delight yourself in the Lord and He will give you the desires of your heart.'*

Scanning the Catoctin mountains to her right, Megan spoke softly. "Thank You, God, for all of my blessings. I've always tried to follow Your word. You alone know my dreams, wants and desires. If my thoughts are pleasing to You, please, please, please, rescue me and make them come true."

Chapter Four

*B*rendon and Megan were sitting on the front porch swing, watching the sun set when Chuck's car pulled into the yard. The man quickly got out and retrieved Taylor's bag from the back. Megan thought it odd that Chuck waved, said something to Taylor and then drove off without embracing Taylor or stopping by to say hello.

When Taylor turned to the house without waving goodbye, Megan knew without a doubt something was off. As her friend trudged toward the porch, both Brendon and Megan walked out to greet her.

"How was your weekend in Wheeling?" Megan inquired.

"Not very good." In the waning light of day, Megan noted the tears on Taylor's face.

Brendon quickly removed Taylor's bag from her hands before taking his sister into his arms. The woman fell into his embrace and began to sob. Megan wrapped her arms around Taylor as well.

"What happened?"

Her friend couldn't speak, but Brendon did.

"What did he do? If that man hurt you, I'll personally make him regret he was ever born."

"It wasn't like that. He told me things need to change and unless they do, he wants some space... permanently."

"Why, and what exactly 'needs to change'?" Brendon's face seemed to be getting redder by the second.

"Chuck feels we aren't spending nearly as much time together as we should."

Oh my goodness! This is because of me. "Bob's your uncle! I'm the problem, aren't I? I'm sorry, Taylor. I didn't mean to intrude into your personal life or be the cause of a conflict between you and Chuck."

"It's not like that, Meg. I guess Chuck is right. I haven't spent a lot of time with him lately, but this isn't your fault."

Of course it is. "Perhaps I should look for lodging in town, somewhere close to school. I don't mind walking everywhere."

"No!" hollered both Taylor and Brendon simultaneously.

"Let me be a man and help out around here a little more," Brendon offered. "I don't mind taking Megan to school or picking her up in the evenings. It will be fun, won't it, Meg?"

Both women stared at him. Megan guessed this was a bit of a shock to Taylor, especially since Brendon had basically ignored her—before Friday. What was curious for Megan was how quickly he had suggested spending more time together. Was it simply to help his sister or was there a different meaning behind his words?

"Would you be okay with that, Meg?" Taylor was searching her eyes. "I don't want you to move into town. What kind of friend would I be?"

Crap. She should have responded right away. "I'm fine with that... as long as it isn't an imposition for Brendon."

"It won't be. Megan and I had a fine weekend, didn't we?"

"Yes, we had fun."

Taylor wiped her cheeks and stared at Megan. "What did you do?"

All of a sudden, it seemed to be exceptionally warm. "We went for a hike and a picnic on Friday evening. Yesterday, your brother took me down the Skyline Drive to a place called Luray to see the caves. This morning, I helped him with chores and your brother rewarded me by taking me out for brunch."

Brendon's sister spun to face him. "Wait! Did I hear this right? *You* went to a restaurant?"

"We went to Mountain Gate, over in Thurmont."

For the first time since she got out of Chuck's car, a smile graced Taylor's face. "You drove over the mountain so there was less chance you'd run into *her*? Smart thinking."

Brendon's face turned pink.

"Her? Who are you referring to?" Megan didn't understand what they were talking about.

"Nobody." Brendon's face was almost fire-engine red now.

"I thought we were chums, or doesn't that apply since your sister returned?"

"Chums? Did I miss something?" Taylor seemed very confused. "What went on this weekend?"

"Nothing," both Brendon and Megan replied, seemingly too quickly.

"I bet." Taylor was actually laughing now. She tapped her brother on the arm. "Would you like me to tell Megan about—"

"No!" The man sighed before glancing at Megan. "I would prefer to be the one to tell her, but in my time, okay?" His eyes seemed to be begging both of them.

"It would be a lot more interesting if I revealed the truth," Taylor quipped.

Brendon sighed and his gaze didn't meet either of them. "I'd really prefer if Megan heard it from me, but can we wait until I'm ready?"

Taylor's smile now seemed sad. "Sorry, I was trying to joke with you."

"It's okay." He hugged his sister again before facing Megan. "It's not that I want to hide my past from you. I just need to think about how to express it. It wasn't my finest hour."

She touched his arm. "I understand. Take as long as you want. I'll wait."

The low rumble of tires on stone drew everyone's attention. A small red Honda slid to a stop before them.

"Who's that?" asked Taylor.

"I, uh, didn't realize you would be here for dinner. Megan and I called out for Chinese. I'm sure there will be enough to share." Brendon walked over and then returned with two bags emitting a very savory scent.

Taylor's eyes were on Megan. "What did you do to my brother this weekend?"

"Excuse me?"

"He never goes out to eat because he says it's too expensive. And now he springs for brunch *and* dinner? Okay, you and me sister, later on, we're going to have to talk."

"About?"

"How did you get Mr. Tightwad over here to chase the moths from his wallet twice in one day?"

Megan felt her smile grow. "I have my ways."

"What does that mean?"

"Taylor, Brendon isn't a bad guy, not once you get to know him."

"But you did the impossible. Getting him to eat out twice in one day?"

"Ahem," Brendon interrupted. "Come on, sis. Don't act like I'm some miser. I can be nice, occasionally."

"When's the last time you bought my dinner?"

"Didn't we stop at the Inner Harbor when Megan arrived?"

"And you stiffed me for the check."

"She was your best friend, then."

"And what, she's yours now?"

"If she keeps doing what she does, she might be."

Taylor's eyes were the size of dinner plates. "Just what did she do?"

Brendon laughed. "Sis, Megan sprang for dinner tonight."

Chapter Five

*O*aturday morning dawned bright and early. Taylor and Chuck had gone away for the weekend, again. Megan smiled as she cooked breakfast. She and Brendon had fallen into a pleasant rhythm. Megan made the morning meal, which all three of them enjoyed together, before catching a lift to school with Taylor. During the day, Brendon focused on the farm work. He was there to pick her up every afternoon. After school, he continued with his farm work while she put together a meal. Some nights they watched the telly or played games. Days when he hadn't yet completed all of his chores, Megan tagged along and helped as best as she could.

After blotting the bacon with a paper towel, she covered it in aluminum foil. Her mind drifted to her co-workers. Several of the female teachers had noticed Brendon's dusty old truck waiting for her after school each evening and were teasing her about him. *They think Brendon and I are a couple—not that I'd mind...*

Glancing through the window, she caught sight of him and his faithful pooch, Orville. They were returning from collecting the eggs. It didn't matter how he dressed—Brendon's muscular outline was apparent. Megan had to be careful not to allow herself to fall for him. Reality waited for her back in the UK—a future void of love or closeness would be her life.

"Good morning." Brendon burst through the door. "Does it ever smell good in here? Is the meal ready or do I have time for a quick shower?"

"Don't tarry too long. I'm about to scramble the eggs."

He quickly headed upstairs and returned just as she was placing the food on the table.

"It smells wonderful. I appreciate you cooking. May I offer thanks for our meal?"

"Of course," she replied, almost automatically reaching for his hand. She'd been amazed at the habit both Taylor and Brendon had of linking hands when they prayed.

"Good morning, God. First of all, I'd like to thank You for the glory of the day and the harvest. Seems like it will be a bumper crop this year. I ask You to watch over Taylor and Chuck, and if You designed them to be together, please bless their relationship. I ask You to watch over my friend, Megan, and help us figure out how to keep her here in Maryland. And of course, I would be remiss not to appreciate the wonderful banquet set before us this morning. Please bless not only the food, but the maker of the meal. Amen."

"Amen. You seem to be in a chipper mood this morning. Any particular reason?"

"Yes. I have a surprise for you. I want to take you someplace I haven't been in years."

"Where's that?"

"There's a giant craft show up in Pennsylvania, just north of Gettysburg. It's called the Apple Harvest Festival." He suddenly grew quiet.

Megan noted a sudden sadness on Brendon's face. "Is everything all right?"

"It just dawned on me when the last time was that I was there."

"When was that?"

"My senior year of high school. I took Noelle there."

"I've never heard you mention her." *Or any other girl, for that matter.* Maybe this is the one Taylor hinted about.

"We had a special friendship—inseparable since we were toddlers. She lived on the next farm over. It's one of the places I now rent to grow crops."

Megan noted a pinkness growing on his cheeks. "You said friendship. Was she your girlfriend?"

"Yes. Even though we never formally referred to our relationship in that manner, we both took for granted we'd be together—forever. We used to talk about where we'd live, what we'd do, which school we'd both teach in, the type of house we'd build and how many kids we wanted."

"What happened?"

After a prolonged sigh, he continued. "Oh, I'm sure you've heard how the story goes. While looking for a rose, I, the world's biggest idiot, allowed the most beautiful orchid in the world to slip from my hands. She was the girl next door and like a fool, I threw her away."

Girl next door? He called me that the other day.
"Did you love her?"

"Looking back, I did—very much. Noelle was so full of life and love and everything good. But I broke her heart. It didn't take long for my ex-best friend Jeff to catch her on the rebound and comfort her."

"I'm sorry. So, she and this Jeff fellow hooked up?"

"They did. They got married right after graduation. The last I heard, they moved somewhere down south. He has a welding business." Brendon shook his head and looked out the window. "I was also told they have four sons and a daughter—and are very happily married."

"I'm sorry. I assume another woman came between you?"

"Um-hmm. But that's a story for another day." Brendon took a deep breath and let it out with a sigh. "Thank you for breakfast. I can clean up and load the dishwasher if you want to get ready."

Megan touched his arm. "If this place has bad memories for you, let's not go."

"It has great memories. That's why I want to take you."

"I'm not sure I understand."

His face had a happy expression and there was something compelling about the tone of his voice. "Maybe it's time for me to step out of this self-imposed isolation I'm stuck in. You never know. Maybe I'll find myself again at the festival. Perhaps it's time to rejoin the living."

Megan excused herself so she could slip on her walking shoes. Her head was spinning. *Am I reading too much between the lines?* Just last week, he had called Megan the girl next door and this morning he used the same phrase when talking about his past love. And then wanting to take Megan to a place where he had sweet memories? *What's happening?*

Another man's face flashed before her eyes, only to be replaced, *very quickly,* by Brendon's.

She combed her hair and used a tie to contain her mane. Pausing, she caught a glimpse of the woman staring back at her in the mirror. In that girl's reflection, the expression was obvious. *Joy.*

"God, You brought me here for a reason. If these things running through my mind are real and true, please allow them to flourish. If they aren't, please move them far from me. And help me discern the difference. Amen."

It seemed as if a hand touched her shoulder, but when she looked, no one was there.

Chapter Six

*B*rendon was enjoying himself. The warmth of the day, coupled with the azure blue of the sky, had him feeling good. *Is that the real reason I'm so happy?* If he was honest, it had less to do with the environment than with the person sharing his day. Megan's eyes seemed to have a certain sparkle in them. An almost childlike aura of wonder appeared to encompass her as if it were a halo. They were visiting the Apple Harvest Festival in Biglerville, Pennsylvania.

"Are you having fun?"

She finished nibbling on an apple cookie before responding. "You Americans certainly know how to enjoy life. We don't have grand events such as these back home."

"This is party central, you know? But you didn't answer my question. Are you enjoying yourself?"

"Of course," she replied with that wonderful accent he was beginning to love. "But the bigger question is, are you?"

"I am." *Because I'm with you.* "So, I was just thinking…"

Megan stopped and turned to stare at him. "Go on."

"I was looking into how you could stay here after your work visa expires."

There was a gleam in Megan's eyes. Was it there because she enjoyed spending time with him as much as he cherished being with her?

"And?"

"There are two possibilities. You did say the kids like you, right?"

"That appears to be correct."

"And you get along well with the teachers and staff?"

"Absolutely, except when they pick on me."

"Do they do that because you speak differently?"

"No. It's because you come to collect me in the afternoons."

Brendon couldn't help but notice how the corners of her lips were curling at the edges. He felt his own cheeks warm. He decided not to go down that path—yet.

"Taylor has been complaining about the shortage of qualified teachers and the difficulty local districts are having filling openings for some time. I just wonder if the school would consider keeping you on." He swallowed hard before continuing. "That way you might extend your visa and could possibly remain in America longer. Maybe even get a green card and eventually become a citizen. And of course, you can plan on staying with Taylor and me for as long as you would like."

"D-do you think the district might do that?"

"Maybe. Look, I did a bit of research and found it's not the date on your visa, but your immigration status that determines how long you can stay in the country." He handed her a slip of paper. "Perhaps the best thing is to speak with an immigration attorney. This one is relatively close by... and besides, he owes me a favor."

"Wait. What? You personally know an immigration attorney who owes you a favor?" The expression on her face changed. "Did I hear you correctly?"

"Well, kind of. Andy was my lieutenant during my second tour in Afghanistan. I got him out of a sticky situation one night. If you're serious about staying, you should speak with him."

"And this man happens to be an immigration attorney?"

"Actually, Andy specializes in elder law—you know, helping senior citizens. But he comes from a family of lawyers and his grandfather owns the firm. When I checked out their website, I discovered one of his sisters specializes in immigration law."

Brendon had expected Megan would jump for joy, but the look on her face confused him.

"I, uh, don't know what to say. I mean, I've dreamed of this, but..." Megan's voice trailed off.

"It seems to be a lot better option than the alternative."

Her face was now bright red. For whatever reason, he was getting a bad vibe of what appeared to be fear.

"W-wh-what do you mean, the alternative?"

"Well, there is another way to stay here."

She shook her head as if to chase away her thoughts. "I'm not following you. What are you referring to?"

He had intended for this to be a teasing, yet tender moment. However, by the expression on Megan's face, Brendon knew he had overstepped his boundaries in a major way. *I should just be quiet.* He turned away from her and pretended to check out one of the vendor's stands. *Why am I so stupid, Lord?* Warm, yet trembling fingers touched his hand.

"I want to hear what you were going to say, Brendon."

"I was trying to be a smart aleck and tease you. I don't think I should. Can we change the subject?"

Megan gently took both of his hands. "First, please tell me what you were going to say."

"I was going to joke with you and say to you that the surefire way to remain in America was to marry an American."

Megan's eyes widened and her mouth fell open.

"I'm sorry. I was just trying to be funny."

"No, I, uh just didn't..."

"It was supposed to make you laugh. I apologize for my insensitivity and stupidity."

She studied his eyes for a long time before replying. "That was humorous, I guess. I, uh, didn't expect you to say that." But the expression on her face didn't appear to relate to humor.

"I guess you got a glimpse of my other side now—my idiotic side. I deeply apologize. I didn't mean to ruin your day."

"You didn't... really. Caught me by surprise, maybe. I wasn't even positive you liked me and then you bring up marriage?"

Wait! She thought I was proposing?

"I wasn't talking about you and me, like being, you know. I just... guess I'm quite the fool. I don't know what possessed me. I was trying to make you laugh, but it was a horrible joke."

Megan's face turned white, emphasizing her freckles. "I understand. Thanks for trying to lift my spirits. Can we do it now?"

Chills ran up his spine. "Do what?"

"Change the subject."

"Gladly." *Whew.* He hadn't known what to expect.

"Okay, but before we do, I want to thank you for your friendship and trying to help me. That last suggestion caught me by surprise, that's all."

"Again, I'm sorry."

"Don't worry about it." A slight blush appeared on her cheeks. "We'll just keep your suggestion in our back pocket for now, shall we?"

Chapter Seven

*O*unday morning dawned with heavy rain. Megan had been awake long before she heard Brendon trudge downstairs. She waited until he departed for morning chores before rousing to start the day. Yesterday had been so much fun, until he brought up the conversation about staying in the States.

Swinging her legs from the bed, she stood and looked in the mirror. *I'm looking at the face of a fraud, Lord. My whole life is one big lie. Please forgive me and guide my future. Help me change my stars.* Megan had panicked during the trip to the festival when Brendon talked about his attorney friend. The conversation had been sweet until he said that trying to get the school to keep her on was a better idea than 'the alternative'.

Stepping away from the mirror, she quickly made the bed. "Alternative? I thought he somehow had discovered the truth." But how would that even be possible? She hadn't breathed a word about the secret requirements in her grandmother's will and what she would have to do to inherit the family nest egg—not even to Taylor. "It wasn't fair what

Grandmother did to me, how she wants to control me from beyond the grave."

Entering the bathroom, she put paste on her toothbrush. Again, her eyes focused on the reflection looking back at her. "I'm sure Grandmother felt she was protecting me, but how could she be so insensitive?" What the older woman had done was to limit Megan's future by placing requirements on where she could live, and horridly, who she would have to marry to receive her inheritance.

The face of George Chamberlain IV appeared in her mind, and just as quickly, Megan forced it out. She concentrated on brushing her teeth. Stories her grandmother had related to her surfaced in her mind. George Chamberlain, *the second*, had been Grandmother's beau until Henry McKenzie swept her off her feet. Then, shortly after the birth of Megan's mother, her grandfather passed away in an automobile accident. Struggling as a single mother with a young child, her grandmother's ex-boyfriend came to her rescue although he was then married to another. It was the beginning of a long-term relationship between the pair. Even as a child, Megan suspected it was more than friendship Grandmother and her old fiancé had shared.

The diminishing roar of the utility vehicle momentarily captured her focus. Brendon was most likely heading to the feed lot to care for the cattle—in the pouring rain. Returning her thoughts to her family, the close association between Grannie and this Chamberlain man again came to mind. The gent supposedly helped her invest and accumulate what

Megan discovered, after her grandmother passed, was a small fortune.

The old lady's regrets at not marrying old George the second had swayed her convictions about her granddaughter's future. The elderly woman had tried time and again to push Megan into the arms of George Chamberlain the fourth. Not that the homely young man would have minded. He leered at her every chance he got, yet Megan successfully resisted time and again.

Quickly dressing for the day, she descended the stairs to brew a cup of coffee. Megan had never been attracted to the man that her grandmother picked out for her. The old lady knew of Megan's dislike of him, but didn't appear to care.

"Marry for money and you'll be set for life," Grandmother always said. "Good looks fade, but money always draws interest."

The woman also despised her granddaughter's obsession with the United States and Megan knew why. Megan's mother had a one-night fling with an American man while on holiday. Mother never told the man he had a daughter because she had no idea how to contact him. Perhaps that explained Megan's deep interest with America. Somewhere in this vast country, her father lived.

The result was her grandmother's deep-seated hatred for Americans. The only exception had been Taylor, from when Brendon's sister taught in Great Britain. In her will, Grandmother had regulated Megan to either scratching out a mere existence on her own or enjoying a life of ease, yet completely devoid of real love. *I can't believe Grandmother dictated the person I had to marry to get my inheritance.* And that happened to be the man who helped Grandmother write her will.

As if that weren't bad enough—the kicker was that the easy life had to be rooted exclusively in London. If she moved from the Greater London area or was no longer married to the appointed man before she was forty, Megan was required to pay back the entire inheritance to the Executor. Oh, and of course the Executor was none other than her lawyer—George Chamberlain the fourth.

Looking out the window, she could see the lights of the feedlot in the distance. Poor Brendon was probably soaked with the way it was pouring. If Megan was honest with herself, she felt a major attraction to Taylor's brother. He seemed to be the perfect man. She had thought that since the day she met him in the airport, when he was holding the sign with her name. He might be gruff at times, but there was something intriguing about him. And over the last several days, the way they had begun to grow close thrilled her. Despite the short amount of time since they began to really enjoy each other's company, she had grown closer to Brendon than any man in her entire life.

But after the event yesterday, the ride home had been silent. He hadn't asked her to tag along for his evening chores and didn't return to the house until long after she headed to bed. In essence, yesterday's problem had deposited Megan at a crossroad. She could either hope she and Brendon could get past the misunderstanding, or she could come clean and admit the truth.

Megan rummaged through the cupboards and refrigerator to extract the ingredients for not only breakfast, but lunch as well. Brendon's favorite breakfast choice was an omelet made with bacon and mushrooms, topped with chives and Swiss cheese... and served with fried potatoes, of course. But since it was such a cold, damp and windy day, Megan thought a spot of soup would warm the soul. She elected to prepare *Aberaeron* soup, a concoction made of beef, bacon, oatmeal, potatoes, onions and a few other vegetables. Her grandmother had taught her how to prepare this dish when Megan was but a child. She hoped Brendon would enjoy the peace offering.

As she minced the additives for the eggs, her mind drifted. "What would happen if I told you the truth, Brendon? Would you be understanding and say the past didn't matter, or would you be cross with me for not admitting the truth? But I guess neither changes the fact—that whether or not I agree with the outcome, my life story has already been written."

Chapter Eight

*I*t was funny how, in the span of one single day, so much could change. Yesterday had been warm, sunny and full of possibilities. The red and golden leaves on the trees had provided a perfect background for a happy day. But this morning, the wind and driving rain had placed a damper on all that was once promising. The weather echoed the emptiness in his heart.

Brendon took his time finishing his chores. It wasn't that he didn't want to see Megan's pretty face, it was that he was ashamed of himself. The visit to the festival had taken him back in time. Joy and happiness were emotions he hadn't experienced since his relationship with Noelle... until yesterday. Spending the day with Megan had felt perfect—if possible, even better than being with Noelle. That was, until he messed it up by trying to be cute and witty. He hadn't meant for it to come out as a baseless marriage proposal, but it had.

The look on the British lady's face hadn't been one of pleasure after he opened his mouth. But it made things a little clearer. The English woman obviously didn't feel the same way he did.

He'd been angry with himself last evening. Brendon had done enough damage, so he remained outside long after Megan's bedroom lights went out. *Well, I'm making progress.* At least Trina hadn't been the cause of his downfall this time.

Trina's beautiful image came to mind, but he didn't allow it to remain there for long. Brendon had never met a woman as beautiful as her, nor one with such an uncaring heart. If he was honest with himself, Trina had been the real reason he'd joined the Army and volunteered for back-to-back combat tours in Afghanistan.

"Enough!" he yelled loud enough to startle Orville. The dog walked over and licked his hand. "Trina doesn't get to monopolize my thoughts. I am not going to waste the day reliving my past mistakes, am I, boy?" As if in agreement, the dog wagged his tail.

Glancing at the house in the distance, he wondered what she was doing. Megan didn't have much of a social life and he felt bad at the thought of ignoring her. It hadn't been the young woman's fault that he was such an insensitive fool.

"It's been a day. Maybe she'll have forgotten the whole debacle." *Yeah, right.* The poor girl probably couldn't wait to return home. All she wanted to do was come to America and have a great time, but what happened? *She got stuck with me.*

The rain slowed a bit to a leaky drizzle. The lull was the perfect time to head inside. Orville jumped in the back of the Gator and placed his head on Brendon's shoulder. "I'll have to judge her mood. Maybe a second apology might set things right." But he couldn't hide the disappointment in his heart. *Just yesterday I believed we were on the verge of discovering something special.*

The rain had picked back up by the time he parked the utility vehicle in the equipment shed. His wet clothes were thoroughly soaked when he made it to the porch. The final layer of moisture came when Orville shook his fur.

"Thanks, buddy."

The dog plopped down on the pet bed and thumped his tail. Brendon reached for the knob, but the door flew open. Standing before him was Megan, but he couldn't read the expression on her face.

"Hurry! Come in before you catch a cold. Breakfast is ready and I've got a hot cup of coffee waiting for you."

What? It took a few seconds to get a response together. "Uh, good morning. You seem quite chipper."

"Three cups of café mocha can have that effect, you know?"

"I guess they might." *Before I address the elephant in the room, I need to gauge the situation.* "How are you today?"

A cloud seemed to cover her face. "I'm okay. I think you and I need to talk, but let's do that after we eat." Her eyes scanned him head to toe. "You, sir, are thoroughly wet. Why don't you get changed while I put breakfast on the plates?"

"Uh, okay. Sounds good." As he climbed the stairs, his hopes dropped. Megan hadn't forgotten yesterday. He had two choices—he could either remain quiet and allow her to put him in his place...

or tackle the problem head first while praying for a miracle.

He changed and descended the stairs. The luscious aroma of eggs and bacon filled the house. Walking into the kitchen, the first thing he noticed was Megan's pretty face. The table was set and she had a coffee cup pressed to her lips.

"The food smells great. Thank you for cooking breakfast."

"You're welcome. Would you prefer to say grace or would you like me to?"

"If you don't mind, I want to."

She nodded her approval. He reached his hand across the table. After the slightest hesitation, Megan wrapped her fingers in his.

"Good morning, Father. Thank You for the gift of rain this morning. Not every day can be all sunshine or we wouldn't have a bountiful harvest. Please watch over Taylor and Chuck and help them resolve their issues. I would also like to thank You for bringing Megan to America. It's funny, despite the three thousand miles we live apart, you brought us together to be friends. I ask You to bless our friendship and always allow us to remain close, if that is Your will. Lastly, thank You for the food and the maker of this wonderful breakfast. Amen."

"That was nice, although I think you better be careful."

What? His entire body heated. "Did I say something wrong?"

"Lying is a sin, and you, sir, are playing with fire."

"I'm not sure I understand." He couldn't tell, but it seemed a smile was pulling at her lips. "Could you explain?"

"Wonderful breakfast? You, sir, haven't even sampled it yet. I think you might have stretched the truth a tad."

Oh, so she wants to play? "I am entitled to my own thoughts, right?"

"I suppose." The smile seemed to fizzle out. "Now, about yesterday..."

Okay, moment of destiny. Help me say this right, Lord.

"What happened yesterday was totally my fault and I'd like to explain. That was the first time I've been to the Apple Harvest since Noelle broke up with me. That long ago day was the highpoint of my life." He was watching Megan for a reaction, but he didn't detect one.

"Go on."

"Being with you yesterday, it took me back in time and, well, it was as if I woke up and everything was the same as it was back then."

"Do I have this right? You pretended I was Noelle? Is that what brought out the whole marrying an American thing?"

"No, that's not what I meant at all. Let me explain what I'm trying to say."

"I'm waiting."

"Noelle was my girlfriend, yes. But she was more than that. She was my best friend, and yesterday, you made me feel like she did. Your friendship, it kind of, I don't know... It made me feel something I hadn't felt in years."

The touch of her hand on his arm startled Brendon. "Can you explain what you experienced?"

"The warmth of your friendship was so comforting. For the first time in forever, I felt whole."

A smile slowly wiped across her face. "I sensed much of the same."

"You did?"

"Definitely."

"But then I messed it up. I tried to be funny and, well, we both knew it didn't come out that way. I'm sorry."

He paused and watched her bite her lip and focus away from him.

"Is there any way you can forgive me?"

Megan's eyes assessed him. Although he'd seen them many times, he couldn't help but notice not only the depth, but the beauty in those blue eyes.

"I need to say this and I want you to both hear and truly listen."

After a loud gulp, he responded. "I'm all ears."

Her gaze was entirely on him. "As you know, I don't have a lot of experience with men— particularly with romance. I've shied away from such relationships because I abhor the games I've watched other people play."

"Megan, I wasn't—"

She held up her finger. "It's rude to interrupt." She shook her head. "Sorry, I slipped into school teacher mode and didn't mean to." Megan took a deep breath. "I enjoy your friendship, so please don't disappoint me."

He waited for her to continue, but she didn't. "Sometimes, I open my mouth and say something stupid."

"And that's fine. I speak out of turn all the time, so I understand. What bothers me is how you completely shut me out afterwards. To me, that was a mind game you were trying to play. I will not stand for that."

"I wasn't trying to make you feel that way. I simply didn't know how to fix it."

"Clamming up wasn't the answer." Megan paused and took a bite of her egg. It seemed as if she were about to say something—or maybe it was a test to see if he would speak first.

"How about this? When I mess up, what if I were to apologize and ask if you wanted to talk about it?"

She lifted her head and looked at him. "I would really like that. And if I make a mistake, will you agree to the same courtesy for me?"

"Of course." He stuck out his hand. "Wanna shake on it?"

Megan stood. Brendon did the same. "I believe we both want a close friendship, am I correct?"

"I think that's a wonderful idea."

"Then, may we hug on it instead?"

"I'd like that." Brendon opened his arms and Megan stepped into them.

The warmth of her body against him brought feelings he'd long ago forgotten. But the sensations were much stronger than he remembered when holding Noelle.

Megan's words were a surprise. She spoke softly and he wasn't sure if they were intended for him to hear or not.

"God, like Brendon stated, our worlds were thousands of miles apart, yet here we are. I'd like to believe this was Your doing. If it truly is, please bless our friendship and bring us even closer than we are right now, every day. Amen."

They parted and sat back down. Brendon wasn't sure, but he felt as if something momentous had just happened.

It was Megan who spoke next. "Since it's so cold and blustery, I'm planning a special meal for lunch. But first, may I make a request?"

Right now, I'd jump off the Empire State Building if you asked. "Ask me anything you want and it's yours."

"After we finish eating, I'd like to hear more about Noelle—and specifically what went wrong, uh, I mean with your friendship."

Chapter Nine

While Brendon removed the breakfast dishes and loaded the dishwasher, Megan continued to prepare for the lunch meal.

"What did you say you're whipping up?"

"This is Yorkshire Pudding, but I'm making it into bowls for our soup."

He watched as she placed the dough into the cupcake tin. "Aren't they small for soup containers? Wait. Are you trying to tell me I need to lose weight or something?"

Megan giggled. "No, silly. You may have as many as you would like. I could make these larger, but this is the size Grandmother and I always made."

"No wonder you're so skinny."

"I'm not, but thank you."

"I'm sorry your mother passed away when you were young. At least you had your grandmother. Were you two close?"

"At times, kind of."

"Would you like to talk about it?"

She adjusted the controls on the oven. "Some other time, maybe. I thought we decided to talk about Noelle today. Were you intentionally trying to change the subject, or just avoid it all together?"

"No, I agreed to let you know the truth. I've never shared everything that happened with anyone—not even Taylor. Want to sit here in the kitchen or go to the living room? I can turn on the gas fireplace if you are cold."

"Since I'm waiting for the oven to warm, let's stay in here."

They took the seats they had occupied during breakfast. After a lengthy sigh, Brendon began.

"I told you about Noelle and how she lived next door. Being neighbors, she and I spent a lot of time together. When kindergarten began, we were both a little scared. Mom took a picture of Noelle and I holding hands when we got on the bus that first day. She was always there for me."

"I'd like to see it sometime, if you don't mind."

He nodded and briefly disappeared into the next room. He returned with a thick photo album and a thinner book. He moved his chair so they were side by side.

"Here's the photo I was talking about." He paused and Megan knew he was waiting for her to speak.

"You were a handsome young lad, and she—a pretty lassie."

"Thanks." He slowly turned the pages, allowing Megan to view the photos in the book. There were dozens of pictures of Brendon and the dark-haired girl he called Noelle. It was impossible to miss the joy on the faces of the two youths in those prints.

"She was my best friend, Meg. We helped each other get through elementary and middle school. But in high school, everything changed. Boys started noticing Noelle. She went out on her first date with Eddie Thomas in ninth grade. I was heartbroken and decided to ignore her."

"As close as you were, that must have hurt."

"It did. About a week after that date, she came over, got me alone and asked what was wrong. I told her nothing was the matter, but she knew what it was. She asked if I was jealous... and I again lied to her. Noelle saw right through it—not only my untruth, but also my anger and frustration. And what she said next changed everything—for both of us."

He shifted in his chair so they were face to face.

"What did she tell you?"

"Noelle said not only did she feel guilty for going out with Eddie, but she was disappointed I hadn't asked her first. She told me how badly my silence hurt because it felt like we were no longer friends. Her honesty changed our lives. We agreed not to date anyone else. Then, what was innocent friendship slowly evolved into a romantic relationship. By eleventh grade, we began to openly talk about a future together. We planned on going to the same college, becoming teachers and getting married after graduation."

"I'm sorry those dreams didn't work out."

"Me, too. The blame for the end of our relationship is entirely my fault. I told you about the Apple Harvest Festival—the highlight of our relationship. Not only did we have a great time, but on the ride home, we agreed on the next step in our relationship."

"What do you mean?"

"I was going to ask Noelle's parents if I could marry her after college graduation. I was on cloud nine. But everything changed the next day."

"Did she have second thoughts?"

"No. There was another girl we went to church with who was in our class. Her name was Trina Lewis." Brendon set down the album and pulled out the thinner book. He leafed through the pages until he found what he was looking for.

"This," he said while pointing at a black and white photo of a beautiful blonde girl, "is Trina. High school homecoming queen, head cheerleader, valedictorian, Miss Popularity, you name it—that was her. Trina was the most beautiful girl in school. Her father owns several car dealerships in the county, so she was rich to boot. Near perfect, on the outside, but in reality, Trina was a spoiled brat who always got what she wanted. And for whatever reason, on the Sunday after our trip, Trina decided she wanted me."

Megan recognized the face from the book. She had noticed the woman in church when Taylor took her there. The lady in the picture sang in the choir. Her face hadn't changed a whole lot from the yearbook photo.

"How did you know that?"

"After the Sunday morning service, Noelle went to visit the ladies' room. Trina walked up and struck up a conversation. We ran in different circles, but had one class together—Trigonometry. She told me she was struggling and asked for help. Being the noble young man I was, I agreed to come over that evening to help her. But when I got to her house, I soon discovered it wasn't tutoring she wanted. Trina told me she had been secretly admiring me for years and my visit was a dream come true for her. Like a fool, I fell for it. When we said goodbye, she kissed me in a very passionate way."

Megan's heart went out to Noelle, even though she had never met her. "Did you tell Noelle what happened?"

"No. I was confused about my feelings. I loved Noel, but there was something so intriguing about Trina. I began going over to her house several times a week, and sometimes, we never got around to trig. About two weeks in, Trina told me she was in love with me. And like the jerk I am, I believed her words. Trina spoke of a future filled with excitement and luxury—one she said we could share together."

"And you fell for it?"

"Hook, line and sinker."

"When did Noelle find out?"

"She suspected something was up. Not only was I not hanging out with her, I was spending all this time 'helping' Trina. I lied my way through it. Noelle found out when Trina told her to let go... because I belonged to Trina now."

Megan couldn't help but notice the solitary tear running down his cheek. She blotted it with a napkin. "How did Noelle react?"

"She cut me off."

"I beg your pardon?"

"She refused to talk to me, wouldn't see me, returned everything I'd given her over the years. I got mad at her and, because I was," Brendon made air quotes, "'in love' with Trina, I failed to try and make it right. A month or two later, my best friend—now ex-best friend, Jeff—started seeing Noelle. They became an item immediately and got married right after we graduated."

"I'm sorry. What happened with Trina?"

"Things went well until Valentine's Day. She decided to start seeing someone else and our relationship faded. In April, I found out Jeff and Noelle were engaged, I knew I'd messed up royally. That was when I decided to forget about college and go into the Army. I couldn't really show my face around town, could I? Everyone knew I was the grandest fool of them all. And I certainly didn't want to be in town when my Noelle married another man. I left for boot camp the day after graduation."

Megan brushed the hair from his eyes. "That had to be a horrible experience."

"It gets worse."

Chapter Ten

" *What* do you mean—it got worse?" Megan was staring at him, brows furrowed.

"My first enlistment was almost over. I planned on re-upping and becoming a career soldier. That is, until Mom wrote and told me about Dad. He had cancer and it didn't look promising. I mustered out of the service and came home. I took care of the farm so Dad could get treatment and rest. That's when Trina showed up, again."

"What did she say?"

"She apologized profusely for what she'd done and begged me to take her back. Like an idiot, I did. She supported me and was at the house almost nonstop to help Mom with Dad. Everything was going great for a while until I found out she was seeing another man on the side. We broke up. Two months later, she was back in tears, begging for forgiveness. Trying to follow Jesus's example, I forgave her."

Megan touched his arm. "Let me guess, she did it again, didn't she?"

"You've got it. And we went through this cycle about five times. The last was the worst. I had been ready to propose to her when I caught her red-handed. I hated her, but one thing I discovered—Trina is my kryptonite."

"Your what?"

"Kryptonite—you know, from *Superman*. The one thing that he can't beat. And that's how Trina is to me." *I'm such a fool.*

"After hurting you all those times, why would you say that?"

"I can't tell her no. Thankfully, it's been nearly two years since I've seen her."

Megan stared at him strangely. "That's why you don't go out to eat very often, isn't it?"

"Yep. It seemed every restaurant I went to, she would show up. Even after Taylor ran her off."

"Taylor did what?"

"Trina kept showing up here, and of course I was too polite to ask her not to. So, my little sister confronted her. I'm not sure what Taylor said to Trina, but it worked. My nemesis hasn't set foot on our land since."

"Good for Taylor. I always did like that girl."

The oven chimed, indicating the temperature had reached the set point. Megan slid the pudding in, closed the door and set the timer. Brendon had closed the yearbook and was staring at the photo album. He felt Megan's eyes on him.

"Do you still love Noelle?"

"No, I gave that up long ago. What I really miss was the closeness of the friendship we shared."

A look of relief filled Megan's face. "Well then, getting back to Trina. Is she the reason you don't go to church as well?"

He nodded.

"Why?"

I wish I could explain it to you, but I don't understand it myself. "The last time Trina spoke to me, she said in time I'd eventually realize we were meant to be, and I'd come back to her. Trina told me she was waiting for me to be on the same page as her. With our history, I'm afraid she'll convince me that she and I are a great idea once again."

"So then, the farm is your safe spot. That's why you rarely leave it, am I right?"

"Yes. That's how I feel about the old place."

Megan again sat next to him. Brendon's eyes were drawn to hers. Her words were soft and comforting. "You can't live your life in fear. You're a fine man, Brendon. Stand up for yourself."

You have no idea how badly I wish I could. "That's easier said than done. Even though I have no intention of getting back together with Trina, I feel like I'm powerless to resist. That's why I don't go to church or most other places around Hagerstown. I don't want to run into her."

"I think the best way to get past all this is to expose yourself to her."

What? "Did I hear you correctly? I should 'expose myself' to Trina?"

"Exactly. See her about town and ignore the witch. Display to her that she has no control over you."

"But you don't understand. That's when I fall for her."

"Well, *we* just won't let that happen anymore, will we?"

"I don't get what you're saying."

Megan reached out and pinched his cheek. "I have a plan."

"Which is?"

She shot him her best smile. "You'll see."

***

Megan couldn't keep her eyes off of him. Taylor had been right. Her brother did clean up well. Sporting a lavender button-down shirt, a black tie and a matching black jacket, Brendon looked absolutely charming.

"I still can't believe you talked me into this."

"Going to a house of worship is important."

"I don't recall reading in the Bible that you have to attend church services. Salvation isn't based on your attendance record, but rather on a personal relationship with God. I listen to several podcasts from a variety of preachers weekly and read the Bible each day. I pray every time I'm on the tractor. What more could God want?"

"It won't hurt to be with fellow believers, will it?"

"If one of them is Trina, it will. I don't understand why she goes to church anyway. She certainly hasn't acted like a Christian."

"Be careful there, my friend. The measure you use to judge others will be used against you. And besides, church is a hospital for sinners, not a hotel for saints."

"Sure, it is."

"Do you remember in the Bible when the Pharisees and Sadducees challenged the Lord and asked him why he ate with tax collectors and prostitutes?"

Brendon nodded.

"How did Jesus respond?"

"He told them those who were well didn't need a doctor, but rather those in need did." He pinched his lips together and nodded. "Fine! You win this round."

"It's not a game."

"Feels like it. I mean, why else would I be dressed in my game-day uniform?"

"Because you and a very close friend decided to go to the Lord's house. And, by the way, you look absolutely dashing."

"Well, the best thing about me is the beautiful lady by my side."

Her cheeks warmed. "Thank you, but I'm not pretty."

"Maybe you need glasses. Have you ever looked in the mirror?"

"Stop it. I know it's been a while, but the driveway for your church is coming up."

He harumphed. "Just because I haven't been here in a while doesn't mean I don't remember where it is."

"I wasn't taking any chances."

"Oh ye of little faith." Brendon backed the truck into a space in the last row. He offered his arm, but instead, Megan slipped her hand into his. They were almost to the walkway when he spoke.

"Well, she's here."

"How do you know?"

His feet stopped moving and he pointed to a red Mercedes sports car. "Look at the plate."

It read, '1-TRINA.'

Chapter Eleven

*T*he once familiar entrance to his family's church hadn't changed a whole lot. Taylor had kept him informed of their struggles over the past few years after it parted ways with the denomination and became independent.

A man Brendon had never seen before opened the door for the two of them.

Megan must have sensed his apprehension because she squeezed his hand. They were almost across the narthex when Pastor Rollins stepped from the sanctuary. Their eyes met and the leader's face broke into a wide smile. Instead of the customary handshake Brendon remembered, the preacher engulfed him in a hug and patted his back.

"Brendon, it's so good to see you. I hope you're coming back to the flock."

"We'll see."

The man next hugged Megan. "Good evening. Megan. You must be a miracle worker, getting Brendon Davis to come to church with you."

She still clung tightly to Brendon. "We both decided," Megan responded with a smile, "to come listen to your sermon this evening." She placed her hand next to her mouth and whispered loud enough for Brendon to hear. "I don't believe the poor man gets the full effect when I try to pass on your message."

"Well, in any case, we're glad you're here." The pastor moved on to the next person in line.

An usher handed them the bulletin. The familiarity of the house of worship touched Brendon and he was suddenly filled with sadness because he hadn't attended for a while. That is, until he noticed Trina's father sitting a few rows back from the pulpit on the left side of the aisle.

Brendon stopped at the first open pew on the right, but Megan squeezed his hand so hard it almost hurt.

"Let's sit a little closer to the front." The volume of her voice dropped. "Follow me, please, and don't give me a hard time."

He angrily glanced at her, but those beautiful blue eyes immediately neutralized his temper.

Megan's words were but a whisper. "This is part of my plan and I'm doing this for you, my friend."

Megan led him to the very first pew on the right—directly in front of the choir loft.

Brendon knew when the choir entered, Trina would have a bird's eye view of the two of them. *This is a bad idea. I need to leave.* She would be staring at him the entire service.

"I changed my mind," he said as he leaned over to speak into Megan's ear. "This has disaster written all over it. I want to leave—now."

She took her finger, touched his chin and swiveled his head until they were eye-to-eye. "Do you trust me?"

"Yes, completely."

"Then we'll get through this together. I promise I'll protect you and I won't leave your side."

Megan's smile reassured him, but Brendon felt as if every eye in the church was boring into his back. Once, when he glanced to his left, he found Trina's father watching him with an unpleasant expression on his face. The man probably remembered the last conversation between them—when Brendon had asked for Trina's hand in marriage and Mr. Lewis said yes.

The acolyte walked forward and lit the candles. The organ suddenly roared to life with a song Brendon often hummed to himself—"What a Friend We Have in Jesus." From the corner of his eye, he caught the shimmer of the red and white gowns of the choir as they processed and filled the pews in the choir loft. And front and center in the row closest to him, Trina stood.

It had been many months since he'd seen the pretty lady, but her beauty almost took his breath away. The time they'd spent together over the years filled his mind. At first, the memories were pleasant, but latter ones filtered in and they certainly weren't happy. Like when he'd stopped by her house to surprise her, only to find her arms wrapped around another man.

Tight pressure on his right hand interrupted the trip down memory lane. The song was over. He and Megan were one of the last few still standing. The warmth of Megan's hand brought him back to the present.

Ignoring the area where the choir members sat, he focused on Pastor Rollins and the service. It took everything he had not to find Trina and gaze at her gorgeous face.

He felt Megan's lips near his right ear as she whispered to him. "Don't pull away."

He almost turned to look at his friend, but then he felt it—the young girl's head resting on his shoulder. Pleasant feelings tingled across his body as he closed his eyes. Megan's face filled his mind and took him on a journey where the two of them strolled along a country road, hand in hand. Endless blue skies opened above them and green fields of corn surrounded them. In the distance, an eagle hunted high above the mountain, but all those sights were eclipsed by the wonder of the girl beside him.

Brendon sensed the smile on his lips, but it left as soon as he opened his eyes. Sitting less than twenty feet away, Trina looked down on him from her perch in the choir loft. There was a steeliness to her gaze, but it softened as their eyes met. A smile covered her face until she mouthed silent words—*"I miss you and still love you."* As those words trickled into his mind, Brendon suddenly felt dizzy, but not in a good way.

***

Megan also observed the woman's moving lips and knew the words were meant for her friend. Squeezing Brendon's hand tightly, she removed her head from his shoulder. What she did next surprised even her and would lead to hours of introspection.

Megan's lips briefly touched his cheek and three tiny words slipped out—"I love you."

The man quickly whipped his head to see her. Competing looks of shock and wonder covered his face. The most becoming smile she'd ever seen now appeared. He continued to gaze at her for so long that she had to again whisper to him, "Pay attention to the service." After a wink, he finally looked at the pulpit where the pastor was just beginning to deliver the message.

What came over me? Okay, she kind of felt that way, but was it because of their friendship, or a secret desire for something more?

Megan allowed her eyes to close and a fantasy captured her heart. One where she and Brendon tackled the world together. He came into school and helped her with bulletin boards. She rode along on the tractor as he farmed. But there was more there than being each other's helpmates.

A peal of laughter rang out from the people sitting in the pews. She liked Pastor Rollins' sermons because he frequently injected humor— and she'd missed the quip. But as rapidly as she'd snapped out of her dreams, they came back. With Brendon by her side, they experienced the world. Everything from grocery shopping to dancing under the moon. Every single second of each day, they spent together—if not physically, then in romantic, connected emotion. Just as Paul described in I Corinthians, they truly became one.

Her eyelids opened and the shock of reality took hold. There would never be a real first kiss for them. In a few short weeks, Megan would reluctantly board a plane to deposit her back in less than merry old England, the beginning of a life sentence free from the true love she craved. To a familiarity so different than this wonderful land of her dreams.

Her focus drifted from her bleak future to the people sitting in the wooden row in front of her. And one face in particular seemed to be drilling a hole right through her. The woman named Trina had Megan in her sights, and without a word, threw down a gauntlet between them. The winner would take home Brendon's heart—a prize that was forevermore out of Megan's reach.

The choir rose to begin the closing hymn. Megan pulled on his sleeve. "When they start to process, you and I should leave."

A sheepish grin was on his lips as he collected his bulletin and stowed away the hymn book. She led the way to the outside aisle on the far side of the pew where Brendon quickly took her hand. Together they walked past rows of worshippers with eyes that took them in and minds that seemed to ponder not only Brendon's appearance, but the way they clung to one another.

No words came out as they walked through the parking lot to his old truck. As he'd lately taken to doing, Brendon opened and closed the door for her before hoisting himself onto the seat. A quick turn of the key fired up the engine. Brendon activated the lights and the parking area was illuminated. A sudden flash of red and white caught both their eyes. It didn't take a rocket scientist to know Trina was running toward them.

Megan spun to focus on Brendon's reaction. With a dreamy smile on his face, he waved at the other woman nonchalantly before taking Megan's hand. He winked at Megan. Although her mind protested, Megan's heart won out and she slid across the seat to allow her head to lean against him.

Pure joy encompassed her as Brendon slid his arm around Megan and held her tight. She knew it was wrong, but Megan allowed her mind to return to a make-believe fantasy—one of a life filled with love between them. A world that wouldn't have to face the harsh reality of what was to come. A love Megan realized she wanted, but one that would never see the light of day.

Chapter Twelve

*W*ith Megan snuggled up against him, the beautiful girl's essence filled not only his lungs, but his heart. A slight sweetness of peaches was in the air. *Is it her perfume or just her natural scent?* They hadn't spoken since they left the church, but that was fine. The two of them seemed connected on a totally different level, in a place where words were no longer necessary. *Is this real or a dream?* This newfound closeness reminded him of what he'd shared with Noelle. *Except my old friend hadn't been as pretty or sweet or—*

"You just passed the lane." Her giggled interruption brought him back to reality and the fact was, he had driven right past his property.

"I believe I was a bit distracted," he said as he turned around in the neighbor's drive.

"Oh, so I see how this goes," Megan snickered. "*You* make a mistake, but it's my fault? How's that happen?"

"I didn't say it quite that way, thank you. The truth is, I should have been paying attention to where I was going, but instead, my mind was on you. And just so you know, I liked it."

Megan slid back to the far side of the cab, but took his hand. The Davis's farmhouse came into view, with every window illuminated.

"Did we leave all those lights on?" Megan's voice had a slight edge of concern.

No, we didn't. What's going on? "Perhaps Taylor is home."

"Suppose she's not and it's an intruder? What should we do?"

"Don't you worry. If something's amiss, I'll protect you. Two tours in Afghanistan taught me a thing or two. Personally, I'm betting it's Taylor."

"What?" she asked with her voice dripping sarcasm. "Taylor home early on a Sunday evening? How could that be?" Her tone changed to concern. "Oh dear, I hope she and Chuck aren't at odds again."

"Yeah, me too."

Brendon nosed the farm truck close to the house. An eerie doubt entered his mind. *Suppose it's not my sister?* Before he closed his door, he looked at Megan. "I'll just go check things out. You lock the doors and stay right here."

"Not a chance, pal. I'd really prefer to be with you." He began to shake his head until she again spoke. "Please? I want to go with you. The place I feel safest is by your side."

"Okay. We'll go together." Brendon stepped around the truck and held the door for Megan. She grasped his hand so tightly that he wondered if his fingers would fall off. They had taken maybe five steps when her grip increased.

"Did you see that?" Her voice was low. "The curtains in the kitchen moved and I saw a face peer out."

Brendon's eyes searched the house. "Was it Taylor?"

"Maybe, but I'm not quite sure."

"That does it. You should get back in the truck."

"No! Where you go, so do I."

"Fine, but when we get to the door, stand behind me."

"Why?"

"In case it isn't my sister."

Slowly, they climbed the steps. Before they could reach it, the door slowly creaked open. Megan did as Brendon had suggested and jumped behind him. Brendon tried to pull his hand free from her to defend himself, but Megan was stuck to him like super glue.

"Where in the world have you two been?"

"Taylor?" Both Megan and Brendon asked in unison.

"Okay, I realize I haven't been around much lately, but gosh, where were you? Out for dinner in Thurmont again?"

She didn't seem unhappy, but he needed to make sure his sister was okay. Megan beat him to the punch.

"Is everything all right between you and Chuck? Is that why you're home early?"

"We are absolutely fine. Chuck is going away on a business trip tomorrow and wanted to catch up on his sleep tonight." Taylor's gaze drifted between them. "Where were you guys?"

Brendon felt Megan move so she was standing next to him. Taylor's eyes were now focused on where they were joined together—their hands. Taylor's expression seemed puzzled.

"What happened while I was gone?"

"We went to church."

Brendon picked up the wariness in Megan's voice as she responded.

"Come on," Taylor chuckled. "I don't believe that for one second."

With his free left hand (Megan still clung tightly to the right one), he removed the church bulletin from his pants pocket and handed it to his sister. Taylor glanced at it and then her mouth fell open.

"*You* actually went to a service—at *our* church? You haven't been to one of those in years, despite me begging you to attend." Taylor again took in their clasped hands. "Exactly how did this happen?"

"Megan asked me to go."

"And just like that, you did?"

"She kind of reminded me that even though I'm a believer, attending church helps. Megan compared it to a therapy group for sinners."

Taylor nodded and then stared at him intently. "Was you-know-who there?"

"If you mean Trina, yes she was."

"Did she see you?"

"Of course. We sat in the first row, right in front of the choir loft. At one point, I believe she might have waved... at us."

Taylor's brow wrinkled as she studied his eyes. "I'm surprised she didn't try to talk to you—or did she?"

"We left during the last song. We noticed Trina run out in the parking lot, so I figured I should be respectful to her."

"Meaning?"

"I waved goodbye."

"And how," his sister's voice was softer, "did you feel—seeing her again?"

Brendon turned his head to look into Megan's eyes. At his glance, a smile appeared.

"It didn't bother me one bit."

"Unbelievable."

"Any other questions?"

Taylor's gaze shifted again from Brendon's face to where the two of them were joined. A sly smile filled her lips.

"I didn't see this coming."

For the first time since she'd slid off the truck seat, Megan relaxed her grip and allowed Brendon's fingers to freefall.

"What are you talking about, sis?"

"This is a revelation, you know?" Her eyes were still fixated on Megan. Brendon suddenly felt the need to protect her.

"Why are you looking at Meg that way?"

"I knew she was extraordinary, but I had no idea."

She suspects something happened between us (which it did), but I should allow Megan to tell her.
"Of course, Megan is special. What's your point?"

"I just realized my British friend has a superpower, but I'm not sure if it's besting Trina Lewis..." Taylor's eyes returned to his, "or swaying my brother Brendon's heart."

Chapter Thirteen

After breakfast, Brendon followed Taylor and Megan to the Bronco. While Taylor might be a very close friend, Megan had been annoyed that his sister hung around last evening until Brendon headed off to bed. Megan needed to speak with him. But maybe she needed to have another in-depth private conversation first... with herself.

The man walked her to the passenger door and held it open for her. Out of sight of his sister, he grabbed Megan's hand and squeezed it momentarily.

His voice was low so only she could hear it. "Can we do what I suggested this morning?"

"Um-hmm, I'd rather like that."

As the driver's door opened, he released her fingers. "I'll miss you," Brendon whispered.

Megan silently mouthed the same words and saw his smile grow. She watched as he drew his hand into a fist and briefly held it over his heart.

"See you later," Taylor said to her brother. "Be careful today."

"You too, sis. Don't take any wooden nickels."

"Watch out for those three-dollar bills."

"Bye, now." Brendon closed the door.

As they headed out of the drive, Taylor spoke. "Finally, we're alone. What happened between you two while I was hanging out with Chuck?"

It was suddenly warm in the vehicle. "What do you mean?"

"I was just wondering about the way you two were holding hands last evening."

"I, uh, was scared. Brendon turned off the lights before we left and when we returned home, the house was lit up like London. I was a tad bit worried."

"And holding my brother's hand quelled your fears?"

"Precisely."

"Hmm, inquiring minds are wondering if that's the whole truth."

Megan swallowed hard. "Do you doubt me?"

Taylor's laugh was unexpected. "My brother isn't a touchy, feely kind of guy. And imagine my surprise when I found you got him to go to church with you. Just those two facts alone have me wondering... not to mention the way both of you acted at breakfast... what's going on?"

"W-what do you mean, h-how do you think we acted?"

"The glances, the shared smiles. I think I know Brendon well enough to see what he's feeling."

"How's that?"

"Megan, he hasn't acted this way since Noelle, except for that short period when he mistakenly thought he believed Trina might be the one." Taylor took her eyes off the road long enough to glance across the seat. "Let me make it plain. From where

I'm sitting, my brother is either in love with you or well on the way."

"W-what?"

"I see right through the act, sister." Taylor giggled. "I guess the main question I have is, is this for real or is he simply falling in love with being in love?"

"Excuse me?" That thought hadn't crossed her mind. "Do you think that's what he feels?"

Another laugh. "You would be in the best position to answer that. Of course, maybe I'm asking the wrong question."

"What are you saying? I'm confused."

They had arrived at the elementary school. "Are you in love with my brother?"

Megan's entire body heated. "I'm still not sure why you would ask that."

Taylor shifted into park and turned to see her. "Your face is blood red. Are you feeling ill?"

"Uh, not at all. It's just a little warm in here."

"And you still didn't answer me. Are you in love with my brother?"

"It's not fair to deliver a question like that as you drop me off at school."

"I agree. We can start with that one when I pick you up this afternoon. It allows you the whole day to formulate a response."

"That won't be necessary."

Taylor laughed. "What do you mean?"

"There's no need to stop by the school this afternoon."

"Why not?"

"Your brother will be waiting for me."

***

Megan wasn't entirely sure her feet even touched the ground. All that changed when Principal Andrews stopped by the classroom holding the hand of a little girl. The child was wearing an old dress Megan knew was a hand-me-down. Her eyes were wide open and full of fear as she cowered next to Ms. Andrews. Megan sensed the girl was frightened by the new environment.

"Ms. McKenzie, this is Chloe James and she will be joining your class. Do you have an empty desk for her?"

"We sure do." Megan introduced the child to the class and found her a suitable spot in between two of the more gregarious girls.

"Ms. McKenzie, a word please?" The expression on the principal's face caught Megan by surprise. She thought for a moment the normally stoic woman might cry. Megan followed Ms. Andrews into the hallway and closed the door.

"Is everything all right?"

"No. I wanted to bring you up to speed with Chloe's story. This is her first day in a formal school setting. Until now, her mother homeschooled her."

"Ah, so there might be social challenges. Have you evaluated her academically?"

"I'm pretty sure that won't be an issue." But Megan knew by the tone of Ms. Andrew's voice that something was amiss. "Her mother decided to no longer homeschool because of her health."

"The mom is sick?"

"Very, and from what I understand, it's only Chloe and her mom. No family or friend support groups."

"I see. Is there anything else I should watch for?"

"I think Chloe knows."

"Knows what?"

"Be prepared. She might want to talk about it."

"Can you fill me in?"

"Her mother's illness is much worse than she's told Chloe."

Chapter Fourteen

*B*rendon opened the window and brushed the dirt from his arms. The unexpected warmth had the weather forecasters calling the heat 'Indian Summer'. It had been a productive day. He'd harvested the last field of soybeans. Before calling it a night, he'd transfer the crop from the combine to the tractor trailer. The soybean silos on the farm were full, so this load would go to the mill in Frederick in the morning.

The pickup's radio was softly providing background music. The local country station was playing a love song by Tim McGraw and Faith Hill. The lyrics had him daydreaming about Megan, not that the song made much of a difference. Thoughts of her pretty smile had been on his mind constantly. It was his imagination, he knew, but it seemed the lady with the intriguing accent had accompanied him all day. He'd felt her presence in the cab of the combine and had imagined Megan watching over him while he worked.

A movement by the school door caught his attention. Three women had exited and were working their way to their cars. He immediately picked up on Megan's frown, even from a distance.

Jumping from the driver's seat, he scurried around and opened the passenger door. The women approached. He couldn't quite pick up the conversation, but guessed the other teachers were teasing Megan. Her face was bright pink.

Removing the stained Baltimore Oriole cap from his head, Brendon swept his arm and bowed slightly. "My lady," he began in a tone imitating Megan's accent. "Your squire awaits the presence of the world's most beautiful princess." His friend's face turned from pink to red, but at least her sad expression turned happy. He reached for her hand and kissed her fingertips.

"Good afternoon, kind sir," she said after clearing her throat. The words were loud enough for her co-workers to hear. "And how was your day?"

"It was paltry compared to the joy of seeing your face."

The other two women chortled as they strolled on by. Megan turned and bid them farewell. Brendon was still there to assist her entry into the cab. After shutting her door, he climbed behind the wheel. At the end of the school property, he pointed the Ford toward Hagerstown instead of the farm.

"Were you intentionally trying to embarrass me?"

"Maybe. Did it work?"

"Yes, but why?"

"It gives those two biddies something to talk about. You see," he raised his finger as if to make a point, "I listen to what Taylor says about school."

"And what's that?"

"That teachers like to gossip about each other."

"And making me the object of their jokes is your goal? I don't need to be under their microscope or the topic of their chinwags."

"Chin what?"

"Gossip. I don't like being the center of attention."

But that's exactly what you are becoming to me. "I believe you're already there."

"What does that mean?"

"Come on, Meg—you're beautiful and kind and sweet and you certainly have charisma. Not to mention that cute accent. Your fellow teachers envy you."

"And your actions make them notice me even more, huh?"

He nodded.

"That's certainly not what I had in mind."

"Did I offend you?"

"Not really. It's just I'm not the kind of girl who likes to draw attention to myself. I prefer being more like a background singer, not the lead vocalist."

Once again, my joke failed. I offended Megan.

"I'm sorry. Is that the reason you were frowning when you came out? Would it be better if Taylor came to pick you up instead of me?"

She touched his arm. "Of course not. Rather, something happened today that made me sad."

"Want to talk about it?"

"A new student popped into my class today. She had previously been homeschooled."

"Is she behind where the rest of your students are, you know, academically?"

"No. Chloe's Math and English skills are far advanced compared to the rest of the students. I pity the child because I'm sure today was her first exposure to a group environment."

Brendon's heart swelled as he gazed at Megan. This lady was filled with compassion.

"Were the other students mean to her?"

"I sat her next to Eliza and Cobie, my two social butterflies. They immediately took her under their wings."

"Then, what's the problem?"

"When I took the class to lunch, Chloe didn't go with the girls to the lunch line. Instead, she sat at a table and stared at the floor."

Brendon took note of the shininess in Megan's eyes. He grabbed a tissue from the pack he kept on the seat and handed it to her.

"Did she forget her money?"

"That was my first thought as well. So, I asked her why she didn't buy lunch." Megan stopped to sniff and wipe her nose. "Chloe's answer made me sad."

"What did she tell you?"

"That she and her mom live alone. They don't have a lot of money and her mother couldn't afford to give her an allowance for lunch."

"I think you should make the principal aware of this."

Megan nodded. "I did. We both spoke to Chloe and discovered her mother is very sick."

"What's wrong with her?"

"That, I don't know. Chloe told us that some days they don't eat at all. But I made sure she had food today. I paid for her lunch for the rest of the week as well."

"Let me know how much it costs and I'll cover next week."

Megan appeared not to have heard. "I know the church has a food pantry that could help, but I feel like I should personally do something. God has blessed me, royally, and I feel as if He wants me to help Chloe and her mother, but I'm not sure how."

"Let me know and I'll be right there with you. Maybe we could put together a care package for her family."

"That would be nice," Megan sighed. "And after all that, then I come outside to have you poke fun at me."

"That was not my intention. I apologize. Tell you what—let me make it up to you."

"What do you have in mind?"

"Hagerstown has the coolest frozen yogurt shop."

She giggled.

"What's so funny?"

"You want to ice down the conversation and obviously feel a frozen treat is the easiest way. Tell me, do they serve puns as well, or is that your contribution?"

"Is this one of those times when I should tell you I put my foot in my mouth and ask if you want to talk about it?" He was trying to be funny, but a quick glance noted the serious expression on her face.

"No. That was fine, but there is something serious I really wish to discuss with you."

"Should I pull over?"

"That might be best. I'd like to see your eyes when we speak."

Brendon directed the pickup into an empty church parking lot. Pushing his seat back, he turned to face her. "What did I do? If you feel I was trying to make a fool of you, that wasn't my intention."

He offered his hand. Megan hesitated, but then placed her fingers in his.

"I know you'd never do anything to hurt me." She bit her lip briefly before continuing. "I'd never do anything to intentionally harm you either. Do you believe me?"

"With all my heart." Her eyes studied him and he began to worry about the look of sadness which seemed to creep onto her face.

"You're a wonderful man, Brendon, and... and I'm glad to have met you."

Megan's breaking up with me? He wanted to talk and tell her how they were right for each other and how he'd never met anyone who moved him as she did, but out of respect, he kept quiet.

"I didn't mean to lead you on."

I've got to stop this, right now. It's going too fast.

"I'm not sure what you mean."

"At church the other night, well, er, I didn't mean to say the words that I did."

"What did you say?"

"You know. The words that leaked out after I kissed your cheek. I'm sorry."

Please Lord, don't let this be the end. "Do you regret telling me because it slipped out, or because you didn't mean to say it—just yet or, because I didn't immediately tell you the same?"

"I'm not sure, but I'm afraid my words might change our friendship. That's the last thing I want or need right now."

With his free hand, he touched her cheek. "No matter where our relationship might lead, I hope our friendship will always come first. You did surprise me, but that's okay. Tell you what—let's wait for God to direct us. Instead of rushing into something that could end up with regrets later, let's allow our friendship to grow naturally. Perhaps it will wither on the vine, but then again, maybe it might blossom into something beyond our wildest dreams."

Brendon was amazed by the look on her face. He imagined it might be the same as a little girl that met an actual unicorn in person. Her continued silence bothered him.

"Please tell me how you feel."

"I'm, I don't know, in shock maybe."

"Why?"

Megan looked away. "Look, I'm not good at this. I was only trying to get your mind off Trina."

She didn't mean it. "Hey, if I said something wrong..."

"No, no. You didn't, at all. I just, oh heck. I've never allowed men to know my feelings, but somehow with you, I feel I can trust you with them. I've never had a boyfriend or even a boy as a close friend. I'm in uncharted territory here."

"Then let's build a friendship with a deep, lifelong foundation, okay?"

The smile on her face was becoming. "I'd really like that."

"Good. How about if your closest *male* friend takes you out for frozen yogurt. Is that okay?"

"Yes, but next time will be my treat."

He hesitated because of his thoughts, but decided the time was right.

"That would be fine, but instead, may I make a request?"

"Uh, sure." Her expression was now different, as if she didn't know what to expect.

Here goes. "Let's make an appointment with the immigration attorney. I'm having a hard time imagining life if you go back across the pond."

***

Megan noted her reflection in the mirror as she brushed her hair. After getting that frozen yogurt, she and Brendon had indeed gone shopping. Together, they created a small care package for Chloe and her mom. Tomorrow, she would find out Chloe's address and later in the evening, she and Brendon would drop off the hamper—anonymously. She would also include a note, telling them about the church's food pantry so the mother would have access to free food. Although Megan and her grandmother had never starved, they had known their share of meager days.

She shook her head. "Why did you make life so difficult for us, Grandmother? You had all that money in the bank, yet we lived as paupers. I don't understand what you were thinking."

Maybe she was reading the situation completely wrong, but Megan worried that Chloe and her mother truly didn't have enough money to buy food to eat.

"But with my inheritance, I can make a difference." Megan would make sure that children like Chloe never suffered from hunger—or had to get by wearing second-hand clothes.

In her mind, she considered what Chloe's home looked like. "Is it a run-down flat?" The place where her grandmother raised her had been small. More than once, Megan had seen mice and roaches scurry when she opened a cupboard door. That was no way to live. She hadn't known what to do as a child, but now, with her new funds, she could change it for others.

"I'm comfortable living on my teacher's salary, Grandmother. I don't need a gigantic house, but the money you gave me will make a difference for many others." Again, her student's face appeared in her mind. "For helpless children like Chloe."

A smile of satisfaction covered the face of the woman staring back at her in the mirror. Slowly, a chill overtook her entire body. The funds her grandmother had left came with a terrible price tag. To help others, she would have to sacrifice her own happiness and future.

She heard noises in the hallway. Listening closely, the soft click of a door closing filtered through the walls. Since Taylor had bid her goodnight a while ago, she knew it was Brendon. Megan knew she should keep him at arm's length, but that seemed impossible. When he picked her up after school, she had tried to lie to him about what happened at church.

"Those three little words. Ones I dreamed of saying, but never imagined I would. Why did I open my big mouth?" She *had* meant them. She knew it... and so did Brendon. When he'd asked her about what she'd said, never once did he inquire if she meant those words in her heart.

"Why does life have to be so complicated, Lord?"

She'd met the man of her dreams and knew he felt as she did. But a future between them was impossible. All because her grandmother had sealed Megan's future, specifying where she must live and whom she had to marry.

The secret ate at her like a cancer. She couldn't reveal the truth to either Taylor or Brendon. Both would put on the pressure to try to convince her to stay. But even if she wanted to, Megan couldn't.

"I mean, I would be crazy to turn my back on the fortune I've inherited, wouldn't I, Lord?"

A response seemed to come from deep within her. It was words Jesus once spoke describing the dilemma of the rich. It was the passage from Matthew. *'It is easier for a camel to pass through the eye of a needle than for a rich man to enter the kingdom of God.'* What would happen if she gave up the inheritance and stayed here? *Would a life of happiness and love await me?*

It seemed destiny now reflected back in the mirror. Not only Megan's but the lives of those she would touch.

"Know this, Lord. I'm not seeking the money for me. I plan to put those pounds to good use for the sake of others." Cold reality again set in. A life of personal despair was a small price to pay if she could change the future for others. "Didn't You say there was no greater love than to lay down my life for others?"

Two men's faces filled her mind. One was the face of George the fourth, with his leering stare. She trembled at the thought of his touch. Then Brendon's image overtook it. Megan could sense his love radiating, wrapping around her like a comforting blanket on a cold night. Climbing into bed, she thought of Brendon. *I'm sorry we will never be, my love.* She doused the light and darkness overtook her—not only her body, but heart and soul.

Chapter Fifteen

It was another gorgeous day. Megan was amazed at this land of sunshine. Back in England, the skies always seemed to be ready to pour down rain.

Chuck slid his Charger into an open space. Taylor spun in her seat so she faced Megan.

"Weren't the leaves pretty?"

"They were gorgeous. Is it like this every autumn?"

"Yes, but I will admit the reds and yellows are especially vibrant this year."

"That's because," Brendon laughed as he spoke, "God wanted to put on a show so Megan will decide America is where she should live."

"Brendon..." Megan was sure her face was red as the coat of a Beefeater.

"Anyway, what I was going to say before my older brother interrupted, is welcome to Thurmont and especially to Colorfest. I was thinking we could check out the stands the vendors have before catching lunch. Chuck and I found this restaurant that serves the state's best Maryland-style crabcakes."

"That sounds splendid." Though she would have preferred to walk holding Brendon's hand, she and Taylor strolled side by side. Occasionally, she would catch part of the conversation between Chuck and Brendon. It seemed like they were deep in discussion about American football and some club called the Baltimore Ravens.

"Do you enjoy doing crafts?" Taylor's words kept her from listening in on the boys' conversation.

"I've never had a chance, except for some of the projects I've done with students. Do you do them?"

"Actually, about this time of year I usually go into extreme crafting mode. You see, I make most of the gifts I give out at Christmas. I think I might be making some extra ones this year. Perhaps you wouldn't mind helping me?"

As long as it doesn't keep me away from Brendon for too long. "That sounds like a plan."

"I noticed that Brendon was giving you lessons on driving the tractor the other day. Did you have fun?"

"It was exciting, moving those big bales. I can't believe he let me do that."

Brendon had shown her how to use the tractor to collect the large round piles of hay and stack them in rows.

"I never imagined I would do something like that."

"Ah, the skills a farm girl acquires."

Megan noted the way Taylor raised her eyebrows.

"One never knows when one might need to fill in for a... friend."

She knew Taylor was teasing her. After their conversation Monday morning, Megan had expected to be grilled by Taylor on her relationship with Brendon. But when they arrived back at the farm that afternoon, Brendon grabbed Taylor's arm and they walked outside. He hadn't revealed what they'd discussed, but Taylor never circled back to her question whether Megan was in love with Brendon. Whatever he'd said had made a difference. Taylor simply smiled when she saw her brother holding Megan's hand.

"Is the crowd too loud?"

"I beg your pardon?"

"Come on, girl. Where's your head this morning?"

"I was just admiring all the sights."

"Oh, you have eyes in the back of your head?"

"What?"

"Normally, it's my brother whom you can't keep your eyes off."

Before Megan could respond, Chuck piped up.

"Is anyone else besides me in the slightest way hungry yet?"

"I think lunch would be a great idea." Taylor winked at Megan. "You can sit next to Brendon if you'd like." Taylor lowered her voice and added, "Unless you're tired of him. After all, you spend every minute when you aren't in school with Brendon."

Megan pretended she hadn't heard that.

Chuck led them a few blocks to a quaint restaurant. It was busy and they waited ten minutes or so before being seated. The first time Megan had tasted crab was on the day she arrived in the States, when the Davis siblings took her to the Inner Harbor restaurant in Baltimore. Today, she ordered the broiled crabcake as did the other three adults.

It felt wonderful, holding Brendon's hand under the table as they waited on their food. The conversation slacked off and Megan noted the way Chuck and Taylor whispered to each other.

"It's rude, sis," Brendon said, "to have a private conversation when you have such interesting company sitting at the table with you. Perhaps you could share what you're talking about?"

Chuck and Taylor quickly kissed before Taylor responded. "Good idea. Chuck and I have a secret to share."

Megan's face heated as a rogue thought entered her mind. The memory of all that time Taylor had spent at Chuck's place came to mind. *Are they going to tell us they're expecting?*

Chuck stared right at Megan and asked. "Are you okay? Your face is flushed."

"No, I'm fine—really. I'm simply anticipating hearing what the secret is, that's all."

"I guess we should confess what we were doing all those long nights I kept Taylor away from home."

Megan glanced at Brendon. His complexion had paled and his hand trembled within her grip. "Okay?"

Taylor laughed. "Tell them the news first."

"Fine," Chuck replied. "Your parents are coming home for Christmas, right?"

Brendon hesitated. "They fly in on Christmas Eve."

"Well," Chuck was the one who was now blushing, "I'm going to ask their permission to marry Taylor."

"The reason," Taylor added, "we spent so much time together is we were deciding whether to keep Chuck's house or look for a new one. We finally determined his place will be fine for a starter home for us. And then, of course, we had to decorate it."

"You're getting married?" Brendon asked incredulously.

"Next June, if Mom and Dad say yes."

"And moving out of the house?"

"Duh, of course."

Brendon stood and offered his hand to Chuck.

"Congratulations, bud. I'll have you know, you are marrying the second-best lady in the world."

"Second best?" Taylor said with a smile. "Who might be first?"

Megan all but melted when Brendon's gaze fell on her.

"What? You don't know? It's Megan McKenzie, of course."

Chapter Sixteen

*M*egan slowly opened the door. Her gaze fell on the field of corn on the right side of the drive. The four of them had watched *Signs* last evening and she was pretty sure she would never walk in or near a field of those stalks again, especially alone!

Glancing at the livestock barn in the distance, she noted the Gator was parked there. Her eyes quickly checked out the roof to make sure no aliens were standing on it.

Now certain there were no extra-terrestrials present, it only took a moment for her to locate Brendon and Orville. The man was feeding the herd. She waited until he looked in her direction before waving. He quickly returned the gesture.

Brendon was a man who followed a set routine, so Megan knew she had thirty minutes or so before he would finish his morning chores. After brewing a cup of coffee, she glanced at her cell. She'd heard the chime earlier indicating a text message, but wanted to be sure neither of the Davis siblings were around when she read it.

Chuck had already stopped by to collect Taylor so they could enjoy breakfast with Chuck's parents, and Brendon would be busy for a while. With trembling hands, she opened the chat feature. As suspected, the message was from George the fourth.

> *"Morning, Megan dearest. It is cold and gloomy here in London this afternoon. Wondering what the weather is like over there. It would be nice to talk to you, but every time I give you a ring, it goes directly to answerphone. And of course, you have yet to return any of my messages. Beginning to wonder if you are intentionally avoiding me. No matter, I'll be waiting when you return to London. Then we can plan our wedding. Can't wait for the honeymoon! Cheerio."*

After deleting the text, Megan shook her head. "Why him, Lord? Out of all the men in the world, why did my grandmother have to pick this *wanker*?"

Dumb question, I know. Her grandmother's biggest regret had been allowing George Chamberlain the second to slip away. Her old beau had amassed quite a fortune and (as Megan discovered only after her grandmother's death) had somehow helped the old lady build a sizeable nest egg of her own. She assumed the older woman wanted to make sure her granddaughter didn't make the same mistake by choosing a man without a sizable bank account (most of which would come from Megan's inheritance).

She shook her head. The one thing Megan couldn't understand was why her grandmother had lived so frugally. Almost all of Megan's wardrobe had been second-hand clothes and she was certain it hadn't been because her grandmother was concerned about global carbon emissions or sweatshop conditions in third-world countries. Why had she acted that way when she could have easily bought the most fashionable clothing from boutiques with spare cash?

Sighing, Megan stuffed the mobile in her pocket. Her mind went to the same place it usually did—to Brendon, or most precisely, to a dream of spending her life with Taylor's brother. A sweet dream, but it could never be more than that. One day, if she did stay and turn her back on the inheritance, this man would come to his senses and get over his infatuation with Megan and her 'lovely' accent. Brendon would surely realize his future would never be a happy one with a plain-looking British girl who had no dowry to offer him.

Noise from outside redirected her attention. Actually, it was two sounds. One was the crunch of tires on gravel. A quick glance revealed Chuck's green and black auto parked out front. The second was the growl of Brendon's utility vehicle. Megan mentally stowed her problems and put on a happy face for her two friends.

It was only a few seconds before the front door flew open.

"Morning," Taylor greeted happily with a huge smile on her face. "Are you ready for church?"

"Just about. All I need to do is change shoes. I worked on packing the sack for the picnic this afternoon. Where are we going again?"

"Someplace I love—Harper's Ferry. The town played a part in our country's history, mainly the

American Civil War, but that's not why I want to take you there. This is where both the Potomac and Shenandoah Rivers intersect. And while the leaves have passed their peak, it should still be quite beautiful."

"That sounds lovely."

She sensed Brendon's presence next to her as Taylor spoke. His warm, calloused fingers walked across the back of her hand, sending shivers of pleasure up her arm. There was no way she could hold back her smile.

"Good morning, Megan. How did you sleep?"

She detected the playful tone in his voice. *So, you want to tease me?*

"Not very well, thanks to you."

"*Moi?*" he asked in fake shock. "Did I do something wrong?"

"That movie was bloody scary. I lay awake all night, worrying about aliens hiding out in your field, just waiting to abduct me."

"Welcome to the family, Megan," Chuck said. "Know what these two did to me the first time we watched *Signs?*"

"Wait! I'll tell," Taylor quickly piped up. Both Taylor and Brendon were doing a horrible job of trying not to laugh.

"I better hear it from you, Chuck, based on the expressions on their faces."

"Right after the movie, these two talked me into a game of hide and seek. It was a dark night with no moon, and of course, Tweedle Dee and Tweedle Dum led me into the middle of the corn field and told me I was 'it'. After counting, I tried to find them, but couldn't. One thing I discovered was that they were great at imitating the bug-like alien voices from the film."

"Why am I not surprised? What happened next?"

"They scared me out of my wits! I got turned around so many times I was disoriented. I ended up at the edge of the field where the woods are thick. I apparently kicked up a deer, although all I heard was something big crashing through the undergrowth ahead of me. And just about that time, your boyfriend grabbed me from behind and screamed 'Gotcha'."

Boyfriend? They believe Brendon is my boyfriend?

"For heaven's sake, quit being a wimp, Chuck. It was all in good fun." Brendon's deep voice was accompanied by his laughter. "If you nice people can give me ten minutes, I'll grab a quick shower, shave and change."

While her friend headed upstairs, the two women finished preparations for the lunch meal. Taylor's focus was on assuring everything was packed, but Megan's mind was elsewhere—on Chuck's words. Although Americans and Brits shared a language, there were many subtle differences behind the meanings of certain words. *Take boyfriend, for example.* The meaning in her homeland meant that if Brendon was truly her *boyfriend*, there would be a romantic or sexual component to their friendship. There was no way she could allow a romantic relationship to develop, nor anything more. After all, she was a lady and she cared too much to hurt Brendon.

"Ooh, we forgot the drinks. Chuck, can you walk downstairs and give me a hand? Be right back, Meg."

"Why do you want me to come along?"

"That's where Mel Gibson and his family hid during the alien attack—in the basement. And this old farmhouse has a coal bin, just like the one in the movie."

"I'll pass on that," commented Megan.

"Chuck will come with me, won't you, sweetie?"

"Great," Chuck murmured as he rolled his eyes. Brendon's sister turned to face her boyfriend with her hands on her hips. Megan picked up on the look Taylor shot at Chuck. "Coming, dear."

The couple disappeared through the cellar door. From somewhere upstairs, the sound of running water could be heard, but if she listened closely, Megan could pick up Brendon's voice. The man always sang in the shower. *Another thing I love about him... and will miss.*

The wave of sadness struck her like a hurricane. She moved to the sink so she could grab a paper towel to blot her eyes. *Why did you stick me in this situation, Lord?* Everything she'd dreamed about her whole life was right before her, but would never be hers. A life in America was out of the question, just like the future she dreamed of with Brendon. Her story had already been written. She would be stuck in London with a loveless marriage to a man she loathed. She cringed at the thought of George's touch.

Megan jumped at the pat against her shoulder. She spun and found herself face to face with Brendon.

"What's wrong, Meg?"

"Oh, nothing," she lied as she furiously wiped her cheeks. "Just dreading a return to London."

"What?" His eyes went large and his mouth fell open. "I thought you wanted to stay here. Did you get a chance to contact the immigration attorney?"

"No, not yet."

He held her hands firmly. "Do you want to stay... or am I forcing you? If I am, please tell me. We're friends, after all, and what you want—that's what is most important to me."

She couldn't help herself. She threw her arms around Brendon. "I know. You're such a great man. I'm lucky to have found you."

Megan backed away and held his face in her hands. This person was now the closest friend she had in the entire world. She needed to tell him the truth, but before she could say anything, Taylor's words stopped Megan cold.

"Chuck, are you seeing this? We walk downstairs and what happens? These two start making out."

"Yep," Chuck agreed. "Like rabbits they be."

Brendon winked before reaching for Megan's hand. "I guess we learned from the best, didn't we, sis?"

"What? You didn't learn anything like that from me!"

Megan could detect Taylor's humor hiding below the surface.

"Are you sure? Chuck did tell you he has a nanny cam at his house, didn't he? And how he can access the recordings on his phone, like the ones he showed me last week?"

Chuck held up his hands. "That's enough. We are heading to church, so stop the fibbing and the ribbing and let's get moving before lightning bolts start coming down. If we don't hurry, we'll end up in the front row. Of course, that would be a great place for both Davis kids to sit so you can ask for God's forgiveness, you know, for the way you two siblings act."

"Good," Brendon replied. "I like the front row. That way Trina can get a first-hand view of me with Megan by my side."

Brendon squeezed her hand firmly for a second. The unspoken words of her soul echoed volumes in her mind. *You not only hold my hand, Brendon, but my heart as well.*

***

Brendon had managed to smile, but inside, his heart ached. They were now in Taylor's Bronco on their way to church. *I can't believe Megan is really planning on returning to England.* Maybe he'd overread and over-reacted to her actions that night at the church.

Glancing across the seat, Megan's head was turned so she could look at the road beyond Taylor, who was driving. He couldn't help but be amazed at the beauty of her profile—and the preciousness of her soul. They were still holding hands, but a great distance seemed to loom between them. After their closeness—or maybe that had only been in his mind—how could Megan plan on leaving in a few short weeks?

It was his turn to view the passing scenery while Taylor pointed her Ford toward the church.

Did I push her too hard, Lord? What was the reason she hadn't reached out to his attorney friend?

Maybe I need to give her space. I would never force Megan into doing something she didn't want to do... But even if it means ruining my life by leaving me? His heart and brain argued about that one before they both replied affirmatively. *She has to come first.*

A distinct noise caught his attention. It was from Megan's phone. *A text message maybe?* He'd heard the same sound numerous times before, but his friend always seemed to ignore it. A strange thought occurred to him.

Who is calling her? Does she have someone waiting for her at home? Could that be the reason she's heading back to London? Brendon doubted that. As close as Megan and Taylor were, wouldn't his British friend have confided to Taylor if she were involved in a relationship? And he knew, if Taylor even suspected there was someone else involved, she would have told him. Ever since the Noelle-Trina incident, Taylor had appointed herself as the guardian of her brother's heart.

He felt Megan shift and looked in her direction. He caught the quick brush of her fingers against her cheek. He squeezed her hand gently and was rewarded with a brief but sad-looking smile. The girl again focused on the passing countryside.

"Please, Lord," he mumbled silently to himself, "Cure this lady's sadness. You know my wishes and desires, but this isn't about me. It's about Your plan. Show her the path You have waiting for her. Fill her heart with Your joy and—if it's possible and if it's part of Your plan, please, please, please—let her see I'm part of her future. Amen."

Though it was undoubtedly unrelated, Megan clutched his hand tightly and then removed hers from his—as if she were already distancing herself.

Chapter Seventeen

*T*hey arrived at the church with ten minutes to spare. Megan wanted to check her makeup, so she asked Brendon to save a seat for her. His smile seemed gloomy, yet he replied that he would.

Inside the ladies' room, she noted her eyeshadow was smeared. Luckily, she had the compact in her purse. Megan was almost finished touching up when the entry door swung open. A woman in a red and white robe stopped behind her. Megan glanced up and quickly recognized the lady's face—the woman who ruined Brendon's life now stood behind her.

"Hi," the robed female said. "I'm Trina Lewis and I don't think we've met. I'm not sure if Brendon ever mentioned me..." The reflection in the mirror had extended her hand.

He did. "Afraid not." Megan turned and stared at the woman.

"Wow, what an intriguing accent. Are you Australian?"

"No." Megan took the women's hand briefly and forced herself to be cordial. "I'm not an Aussie, I'm British. My name is Megan McKenzie."

"Ah," Trina replied and a light seemed to come on somewhere under the perfectly coiffed hair. "You're the one I've heard so much about—you know, you teach at the elementary school."

"Yes, I realize that." *Idiot. What did Brendon ever see in you besides the pretty face and the perfect hair?* Megan had never seen Trina when she wasn't wearing a choir robe, but suspected the flowing fabric hid a perfectly-proportioned body.

Trina laughed. "I didn't mean it that way. My father is on the school board and at one of the board meetings, it was mentioned how much the children, staff and parents like you. I guess they see something special in you and feel you reflect positively on the teacher exchange program. That should open the door for other candidates like yourself in the future."

"Thank you." She felt her cheeks warm. Was the lady truly being kind or was there an underlying current here? *Who knows?* Maybe Trina had changed since her involvement with Brendon. *Regardless, always be nice to others.*

"May I ask a personal question?"

"Uh, I guess."

The woman took a deep breath before continuing. "Are you and Brendon involved?"

"What do you think we're involved with?" Megan acted shocked at the question. *Like I don't know what you're asking, lady.*

"You know, like, with each other. The two of you... well, I don't know how to say it exactly, but fine, here goes. Brendon hasn't been at church for such a long time and then, the two of you show up right in front of me with that public display of affection in the first row of church. It was quite the surprise and it makes me wonder… Was it truly love, just a show to get my attention, or possibly something else altogether?"

"Like what?"

"Perhaps you are taking the opportunity to sow your wild oats while you're in this country, which means you're only using Brendon and none of what you're doing really matters to you."

Megan didn't respond, but she noted the deep shade of red growing across Trina's face. It was time to disengage and sail out of there—quickly.

Before she could get out of the room, Trina grabbed her arm and swung Megan around so they were face to face.

"Maybe you didn't know this, but Brendon and I were a couple, for a long while. I loved him then and still do. Deep down inside, I'm pretty sure he still has feelings for me. I guess what I'm saying, Megan, is if you two aren't serious, I'd like to put you on notice. That man's happiness is what really matters to me, so if you're toying with him, step aside. I won't allow anyone to hurt my Bren-Bren."

***

Brendon was becoming concerned because Megan hadn't returned. The organist finished the prelude and Pastor Rollins' opening remarks had been made.

Concern turned to worry when the choir entered, took their place in the loft and finished the opening hymn. Trina had him locked in her sights with a knowing smile on her face. A quick look to his left found Taylor staring at him. She motioned for him to listen to her. He leaned over.

"Let me out. I'll check on Megan."

Both Chuck and Brendon swayed back to allow his sister to pass. Suddenly she stopped. Megan entered the pew and slid next to Brendon.

Taylor kept her words soft. "Are you okay?"

"Never better." There was something strange about both Megan's eyes and tone. To his utter surprise, Megan grabbed his chin and kissed him— fully on the lips! The wet embrace lasted for at least five seconds. This certainly wasn't a kiss 'only friends' would share, but a toe curler like he'd never experienced before. She pulled away and whispered in his ear, "Go with it. I'll explain later."

Megan sat next to him, tightly gripped his hand, and leaned her head on his shoulder. Brendon glanced at Taylor, whose eyes were open wide. Silently, she mouthed, "Knock it off. We're in church."

He could feel Megan's pulse beating where their fingers intertwined. It was certainly strong, but very fast. *What just happened?* His gaze fell on Trina. If looks could kill, Brendon would soon be carrying Megan's lifeless body from the sanctuary.

Trina must have sensed his attention, because she shifted her view to him. In what seemed less than a second, her expression completely changed. An enchanting smile covered those lips and he was filled with a sudden desire to talk to Trina, to hear her voice and—

What am I doing? Am I losing my mind? He shook his head. Without even speaking a word, he could feel Trina drawing him to her.

Brendon removed his eyes from that familiar face and they landed on the top of Megan's head. Her brown hair had quite a few blonde strands as well as a few that were ginger-red. Her mane may have lacked the shiny luster of Trina's silky blonde hair, but there was something Megan had that Trina never would—his heart.

Leaning over, he gently kissed the top of Megan's head, as if it were the most natural thing in the world to do. Much to his surprise, the girl seemed to shudder for a moment, but then he felt it. His friend squeezed his hand tightly for a very long time.

Brendon followed the rest of the congregation when they stood for the final hymn and the pastor's benediction. After the chimes repeated the melody of the last song, the parishioners began to shuffle to the main aisle so they could shake the pastor's hand.

Taylor allowed Chuck to exit from the pew to the aisle before she blocked it. He could tell his sister was quite unhappy. She pointed at her friend's face. "I don't know how you do things in jolly old England, but over here, kissing my brother that way in front of everyone in the church is unacceptable. If you're going to act that way—"

Megan held her hands in front of her. "Please, I'll explain, but this is neither the place nor the time."

"No," hissed Taylor. "I want to know what you were thinking and why you did that. You made a fool of our family." She was pounding her finger into Megan's chest to drive the point home.

Brendon had been watching Megan's face. Her expression seemed ready to crumble and he knew what he had to do. He gently grasped Taylor's hand and stepped between the two women.

"Please, sis. Not here. Let's get in the car before we continue the conversation."

"And of course you take her side. I was worried you were going to start making out."

"You know both of us better than that. Let's table this discussion until we get in your Bronco."

Taylor opened her mouth to say something, but Chuck touched her arm. "Come on, Tay. Brendon isn't saying not to talk about this, he just wants to do it in private. If that was you in Megan's shoes, I'm confident it's what you would want as well."

Taylor closed her eyes and took several deep breaths. The action calmed her and she reached for Megan. "I'm sorry I blew up at you."

Megan hugged her friend tightly. "It's okay. I'm sorry I shocked you, but as soon as we get away from here, I'll spill the beans—I promise."

Brendon was more confused than ever, but he offered the crook of his arm to Megan. Instead, she intertwined their fingers with her left hand and used her right to pull them together so tightly that one couldn't slip a piece of paper between them.

The four of them were at the very back of the receiving line. It was several minutes until they reached the narthex where Pastor Rollins stood. He greeted Taylor and Chuck, allowing them to step aside so the only ones left were Megan and Brendon.

He'd never seen their pastor with as wide of a smile. *I thought he'd be upset that Megan kissed me that way in front of the entire congregation.*

Yet the man opened his arms and pulled them both into his embrace. "This is a miracle. I understand congratulations are in order."

"What?"

"You'll have to allow me to get my calendar before we set the date."

Confused, he looked away from the pastor to Megan. Her face was as red as an International Harvester tractor fresh from the factory. "We weren't ready to go public with it yet. Brendon wanted to tell his parents first before we made an official announcement."

Announcement?

"I'm sorry," the man said as his face paled. "Trina Lewis told me the news you shared with her. I guess she was so excited she missed that last part."

Brendon had no idea what was going on. He touched Megan's cheek. "What did you tell Trina?"

His friend swallowed hard. Brendon knew she was nervous and that the smile she offered was forced.

"Megan?"

"I shared our news."

"Which news?"

"That you and... and I... are e-e-engaged."

Chapter Eighteen

*T*urning out of the church parking lot, Brendon's sister pointed the Bronco in the general direction of Interstate 70. The silence in the cab was driving him crazy. The whole ordeal at the church had him flummoxed to the extent that he didn't even know how to begin the conversation he and Megan needed to have.

Taylor whipped the SUV into a strip mall, and parked in front of a coffee house. "I think we all need something to calm our nerves. Let's grab a brew and then sit at one of the outside tables so we can have some privacy."

Megan touched his arm. "Would you mind ordering for me?" He glanced and found her cheeks were moist.

"Café mocha?"

"Yes, please."

The four left the vehicle and moved toward the shop. Megan veered off, head hung low.

Taylor pulled Chuck in and the two held a brief, whispered conversation. Chuck nodded and walked over to the table Megan occupied. The British girl had buried her face in her hands. Brendon's heart told him he should comfort Megan, right this very second. He took one step in that direction, but Taylor firmly grasped his arm. "I'd like to talk with you, first."

"But Megan—"

"Can wait." Taylor's eyes appeared large and he sensed her anger. *At me or Megan?* Once they were inside, she quickly turned. "Exactly what happened at church? I'm certain our family is the gossip topic of the day for the entire congregation."

"I'm not quite sure. I'm as confused as you."

"Is what Megan told the pastor the truth—that you and she are engaged? I knew you two were close friends, but this is bizarre and completely out of character for either of you." Taylor grasped him by the arms and lowered her voice. "Wait. Did you get her in trouble?"

"What?"

"Is Megan pregnant?"

"Taylor!" Brendon was inflamed. "You know me better than that. If you think I slept with her, you're out of your mind. My view of marriage is a lot like yours, or at least what I thought you believed. That embrace she gave me was the first time we'd even kissed and I would never sleep with Megan or anyone else without putting a ring on the woman's finger first."

"Sorry." His sister closed her eyes and took a deep breath. "I apologize for jumping to conclusions. But tell me the truth—are the two of you secretly engaged? I've heard you tell her several times she could stay in the United States longer if she married an American. Is that what this is about?"

"Megan's comment was as surprising to me as it was to you. We never discussed the subject of marriage."

A look of confusion covered Taylor's face. "Then what happened?"

"Again, I don't know, but by the look on Trina's face, I believe it involves her. She's crazy. Perhaps she and Megan had an altercation and this was Megan's way of getting back at Trina."

"Maybe that's the truth, but I don't know. Let's order so we can find out from Megan what happened."

"What if I order so you can talk to her? Just send Chuck in. I think the two of you should speak before I get there."

"Why?"

"Because she and I need to have a heart-to-heart. I need to think about not only what to say, but how to say it."

Taylor touched his cheek. "You're in love with her, aren't you?"

"When I know for certain, I promise I'll let you know first."

Taylor stepped out and Brendon placed the order. The barista wasn't in a hurry, which was fine with him. Chuck walked in and stood next to Brendon.

"Are congrats really in order?"

"Not that I'm aware of."

Chuck shook his head. "Gotcha. Women sure are difficult to understand. You know, I thought Taylor was a handful, but Megan is—"

"Don't even go there," Brendon interrupted. His voice was gruff, but he really didn't mean to take his frustration out on Chuck. "Sorry, but I don't want to hear you run either of them down. Both those ladies are special to me."

"My apologies." Chuck stepped away from the counter and found a seat at an open table.

What in the world happened between the time we arrived at church and her appearance in the pew? Brendon suspected Trina had done something to force Megan to react the way she did. But kissing him that way, in church? Not that he minded, but still. He'd dreamed about what it would be like to touch Megan's lips... and the actual event was better than he'd imagined. However, the time and the place were confusing. *It had to be Trina!*

The barista brought one solitary cup to the counter. "Earl Grey with two Splendas and half and half?"

"I'll just wait until you make the other three before I take them."

"Suit yourself." The woman adjusted her nose piercing and then returned to the preparation area. Brendon breathed a sigh of relief when the girl used hand sanitizer before working on the next beverage.

"You know, Lord, if she said that so she could stay, I'd be okay with it. If Megan's announcement was because she loved me and wanted this, I'd be overjoyed. But just this morning, she was sad because she told me she was returning to England soon. I'm utterly confused. Please help me understand, and I'm not talking about what she said, but her real feelings. Is she interested in me or is everything one big lie?"

***

I wish I were in London right now. Perhaps she should pull up stakes and leave tomorrow. However unappealing the thought might be, George was waiting on her. They could get the inevitable over and she could begin her life anew. *Something to look forward to, isn't it?*

A warm touch against her arm startled Megan so much that she jumped back—Taylor.

"Meg, it's okay. It's only me."

She wiped the frustration from her eyes. "I didn't mean to make fools of either you or Brendon. I'm so sorry."

"It's fine," Taylor murmured kindly as she helped wipe away the tears. "Brendon and I figured out that something happened, didn't it?"

"Yes," she mumbled softly. "And now I've messed up everything."

"Trina had a part to play in this, didn't she?" Megan nodded her head. "Tell me what happened."

"I was touching up my makeup when she walked in. She introduced herself and then it was as if something snapped in her. She wanted to know what was happening between Brendon and I."

The odd look on Taylor's face made her shudder. "What is going on with you two?"

Megan ignored the question. "Trina asked whether it was real or an act or something else."

"Like what?"

"She accused me of using your brother to sow my wild oats. If Trina knew me, she'd understand I'm not that kind of girl."

"You aren't, but she is. She's shown that side of herself to Brendon time and time again." Taylor paused. "What happened next?"

"She told me that if we weren't madly in love, she would find a way to, how did she say it? That's right—win back the man God made for her. And that's when I messed up."

"What are you talking about?"

"I blurted out that Brendon and I were engaged. She laughed and called me a liar."

"That was rude. Why would she say that?"

"The witch grabbed my left hand and said, 'If you're engaged, where is the ring?' Remembering why you aren't wearing one yet, I used the same excuse—Brendon is waiting to talk to your parents first. I'm sorry I failed you." It was becoming hard to see clearly.

"Don't worry about it." Taylor giggled and Megan stared at her.

"What's so funny?"

"Oh, nothing."

"That's not fair. Tell me your thoughts."

"It's kind of cool, even if it is just pretend, to think of you as my sister-in-law."

Chapter Nineteen

*D*uring the drive to the National Park in Harper's Ferry, Taylor had reiterated what happened between Megan and Trina. Brendon listened to his sister's explanation and wondered at Megan's silence. Even more disturbing was that when he offered his hand during the drive, Megan simply looked away and didn't touch him.

Once outside the vehicle, Brendon helped Chuck carry the supplies to a picnic table overlooking the Shenandoah River. His eyes were on Megan as she stood forty feet away, arms crossed and head facing the spot where Maryland, West Virginia and Virginia intersected.

His heart was breaking. The distance between them in the Ford might have well been the same as between Hagerstown and London. This wasn't even his fault. *Trina strikes again and who ends up the big loser? Me.*

"What are you doing standing here?" came the whispered question from Taylor.

"Is there something you need me to do? I thought we brought everything out of the Bronco."

"Don't play dumb with me. Why aren't you over there with Megan?"

His eyes engaged hers. "And what exactly do I say? Sorry you told a fib?"

"No. Don't rub her nose in it. She's suffering enough right now. You do realize she said what she did to protect you, don't you?"

"And now this is all my fault?"

Taylor shook her head. "I didn't say that. Megan tried to shelter you from Trina. Okay, maybe that wasn't the brightest move to make..."

"Ya think?"

"Quit acting like an idiot. She's hurting. Go comfort her."

"And still, I'm at a loss for exactly what I should say or do."

"Are you the same man you were this morning or did you lose your soul?"

"What? Why would you even say that?"

"You always know what to do to help others, so why is it different with Megan?"

"Look Taylor, I don't have a clue even where to begin."

"The Army gave you a bronze star for bravery. I believe the award stated that you put your life on the line when you rescued three wounded soldiers while under intense hostile fire. Had the Army trained you on *exactly* what to do in that particular situation, place and time?"

"No, we never trained on that precise situation, but I was trained on how to adapt to unexpected situations."

"Then go do the same thing now. Improvise."

He continued to stare at his sibling. She finally shoved him.

"Get moving. Be the man your dog thinks you are."

Reluctantly, Brendon walked to where Megan stood. He could see the moisture on her cheeks.

"Megan?"

"I'm sorry." Her words came quickly. "I didn't mean to act stupid and I know I hurt you. I think it would be best for everyone if I packed tonight and caught a jet home tomorrow."

He gazed into her eyes and everything inside him changed. What would his world be like if Megan did just what she said? *I can't let it end like this.* From out of nowhere, the answer became crystal clear.

"Don't do that. I don't want you to leave. I need you to stay, please?"

The woman shifted to see him clearly. "Even after all this? I'm sure you hate me right now."

He took her hands, which were ice cold. "I could never feel that way about you. We're friends. Taylor shared that you said you did it for me. Just so you are aware, I appreciate your kindness."

"Right, and won't this all just be a bloody mess for you when I'm gone?"

Then I'll convince you to stay—just watch me. "We'll worry about that when the time comes. But for right now, we've got something more important to discuss."

Megan wiped her cheeks with her hands. "What are you talking about?"

"Why, my dear. You are my fiancée." A gentle nudging within Brendon drove him further. "I think we need to explore how we can become even closer."

"This isn't making sense," Megan said as she stared at him. "I served up the biggest dog's dinner in human history and you want to know how to become closer?"

"Wait! You fed Orville? Like before we left or do you have some mind over matter skill that you can feed my pooch without being home? That would be a breakthrough in the metaphysics world. This is earth-shattering! We might be able to make a fortune off of this." He knew what she had meant, but his comment had the intended effect. Brendon had brought a slight smile to her face.

"Quit being a jerk. You know what I mean."

"Not a clue. Hey, I've got a thought."

"What now? I'm almost afraid to ask."

"Let's go have lunch. I understand both you and Taylor packed the goodies."

As she stood there considering his offer, she swiveled slightly, almost as if she were dancing. "That might be nice. I did make the shrimp salad—just for you."

"Then what are we waiting for?" But when Brendon extended his hand, Megan's smile left. She didn't reach for him. His voice was softer when he spoke again. Based on what she'd shared in the past, Brendon believed he could read her mind.

"No games, Megan. This is the hand of friendship. The engagement announcement might not have been real, but this, you can count on. We'll always be friends—first and most importantly. Anything else, real or pretend, will never measure up to our friendship. And I hope we never allow this to fade."

Megan studied him for a long time before touching him. The tender expression on her face warmed his heart.

"I'm glad I met you."

"You better be."

"What?"

"I hope you're happy having me as a friend, you know, considering we're engaged and all that."

Megan threw her arms around him and hugged him tightly. "Thank you for not being angry about all this."

"Nonsense. We'll manage together, *honey*."

Megan slowly relaxed the hug so she could see his face. "Honey?"

"Well, we are engaged, right? We should have some term of endearment for each other, you know, for everyone else's sake. If you don't like honey, would you prefer I call you something else? There's peach, buttercup, sunflower, sugar pie—the list goes on and on."

"I rather prefer honey. But what should my name for you be?"

"I don't know... something cool, like sport or champ. Back in my army days, they called me bubba."

Megan wrinkled her nose as she took him in. "Hmm, somehow bubba doesn't sound like something I'd say. Maybe sweetheart or darling. Do you have a preference?"

"No, honey."

"All right then, *darling*. I believe I'm ready for lunch."

She began to walk away, but he remained where he was standing. "One more question."

"Yes?"

"Was there any thread of truth in what you told Trina? I mean, if things were different, you know... would I be the type of guy you'd like to be engaged to?"

She squeezed his hand tightly and gave him a wink. "Did you even have to ask... darling?"

Chapter Twenty

The last twenty-four hours had been a whirlwind for Megan. After the flub-up in church, Taylor had driven them to Harper's Ferry. *I'll always remember yesterday.* Her tiny white lie could have been devastating to their relationship, but Brendon had graciously let her off the hook. Not only had he forgiven her, but the friendship they shared had grown deeper. After returning from the picnic and the completion of his chores, Brendon took her to the cinema to watch a romantic comedy.

The bell rang, signaling the end of recess. Luckily, this wasn't her day for playground duty.

Last evening had been perfect, well almost. After the show, Brendon had walked her to her bedroom to wish her goodnight. At the threshold of her room, the man had touched her cheek and softly spoken her name. Megan knew exactly what he wanted—a kiss like she'd given him at church. The memory of that moment made her face warm. *I'll think of that later.*

The first squeals of the children in the hallway told her they were returning from outside. Megan allowed her mind to return to last evening and

Brendon. There was nothing she would have liked better than to kiss him without anyone around, but instead of finding her lips, he'd pressed his to her forehead. Something had changed within him and Megan couldn't allow herself to believe those thoughts might actually be real.

The rest of the morning class activities passed quickly and before she knew it, it was time for lunch. At the appointed hour, she walked her students to the cafeteria. And she made sure Chloe had a tray full of food.

Lunch was pizza, something Megan didn't have the same enthusiasm for as most Americans. Carrying her tray to the faculty table, a sudden movement caught her eye. A man wearing a brown uniform was being escorted by the school secretary, Sylvia Plum. Megan sat down and her eyes followed the man as he approached. His trajectory appeared to be her table. As he advanced, she noted the long, manila-colored box he carried. The pair stopped in front of where she was sitting.

"Here she is," Ms. Plum announced. "This is Ms. McKenzie."

The older man offered a pleasant smile. "And these would be for you." He offered the almost meter-long box to Megan.

"Thank you. What is it?"

"Open them, ma'am."

Megan did as he suggested and removed the lid. Her heart caught in her throat as she gazed at the large bouquet of yellow roses. "Oh my. Aren't they wonderful? They're my favorites."

"Who are they from?" asked Ms. Plum.

"There is a card attached to the exterior of the box," the delivery man offered in a helpful manner. But before Megan could retrieve it, fifth-grade teacher Gabby Starrett grabbed it and opened the envelope.

"Please hand that back to me."

"Your hands are full. I'll read it to you."

"Please don't."

"Dearest Megan, my honey. These flowers may be beautiful, but they could never hold a candle to you. I can't wait to see you this afternoon. Thank you for being my fiancée. Love, Brendon."

"Fiancée?" everyone at the table asked at once. Megan's face was on fire.

"Wait," Ms. Starrett said. "Who are you engaged to?"

"Duh," Ms. Plum answered. "It's obviously Brendon Davis. You must have seen him waiting to pick Megan up every day after school."

"Brendon? What a hunk," exclaimed Ms. Starrett. "Have you checked out the arms on that man? Either he works out constantly or—Wait! You're not wearing a ring. What gives? If that was me, I'd be showing the ring off to everyone I meet."

"We, um, Brendon wants to let his parents know first before we publicly announce it."

"When will that be?" Music teacher Angie Levitt joined in the conversation. "Why couldn't he do a video chat with them?"

"Brendon is a little old fashioned."

"Where did he propose to you?" Ms. Plum asked.

Oh, crap. What do I say? She quickly ran through the memories of the places he'd taken her. One stuck out in her mind. "Brendon proposed at Cunningham State Park, beside the falls."

"Tell us how he did it." Ms. Levitt shared a devious expression with the others at the table. "We want to know all the juicy details."

Think, mind, think. "It was a sunny day and we were walking hand in hand..." What she told them was a mixture of half-truths about their times together and her dreams of what a real proposal would be like. As the words came out, Megan was drawn deeper and deeper into the fantasy—that all this was real and Brendon was hers.

The bell signaling the end of lunch interrupted the story.

"We'll pick up on this tomorrow," Ms. Starrett said.

"I can't wait to hear about the wedding plans," Ms. Levitt added. "It will give me ideas for my own wedding, someday."

"You better find a man, first," Ms. Starrett countered.

"I just hope he's better than your ex."

Megan's class wanted to know what was in the box, but she managed to fend off their questions with a stern, "Never you mind."

All that changed when Ms. Levitt arrived for music session.

"Good afternoon, class."

"Good afternoon, Ms. Levitt."

"Today is a special day and we're going to celebrate. Does everyone know how to sing the Happy Birthday song?"

Megan felt her temperature rising. *Please, no.* She had to stop this.

"Ms. Levitt?" The young blonde ignored her.

"I found out today that Ms. McKenzie just got engaged."

"What does that mean?" asked one of the boys.

"Is it contagious?" asked another.

"No. Being engaged means Ms. McKenzie is getting married."

The boys and girls started asking a thousand questions all at once, such as who she was marrying and when she would have children.

The humiliation continued while Ms. Levitt instructed and then led the children in singing a happy engagement song. Following the public embarrassment, the music teacher got on with her lesson.

Finally, she was finished. Megan walked the other teacher to the hallway. "Thank you, Ms. Levitt, but that was quite unnecessary."

The young woman had stars in her eyes. "I envy you, Megan. From what I've experienced, there aren't many good guys out there. But I believe everyone would agree, you found a gem in Brendon Davis."

"I did, thank you."

"I do have one question, though. Aren't you concerned about the age factor?"

"Excuse me?"

"He's got to be, what, twenty years older than you?"

Megan didn't even know how old Brendon was or when his birthday was. *Does age really matter?* She realized Ms. Levitt was waiting for an answer.

"You know the old adage... love is blind."

"Aw, how sweet."

"I must be getting back to my class."

"One more quick question."

"What is it?"

"Will you be taking his name or keeping yours?"

"I beg your pardon?"

"Will you stay Ms. McKenzie or will you become Mrs. Megan Davis?"

Chapter Twenty-one

$\mathcal{T}$he soybeans had all been harvested. It was time to get ready for picking corn. That meant changing the attachment on the front of the combine. Considering it had been a year since he'd last had the corn picking attachment in operation, Brendon decided to service it first.

He climbed up on the unit and was using a grease gun to lubricate one of the bearings when his foot slipped. His arm smacked hard against the steel head and he continued to fall. As he stuck his hand out to prevent himself from hitting the ground, his skin caught on a sharp edge of metal. The resulting injury was a slice about eight inches long on his left arm. It not only hurt, but it bled like crazy.

"Great," he exclaimed. Being a farmer, Brendon was used to the occasional cut, bruise or scrape. He walked over to his toolbox and extracted the first-aid kit. After opening it, he shook his head.

"Doesn't that beat all?" Brendon had forgotten to restock the kit after the last time he used it. Not wanting to take the time to return to the house for supplies, he did what any red-blooded American farmer would do when he was in a pinch—he used duct tape to close the wound.

By the time lunch rolled around, Brendon had the combine's corn head attached and ready to go. He relocated the massive machine to the first field of corn to be harvested and then shut down the John Deere.

Brendon was whistling as he walked back to the equipment shed so he could drive the grain truck into the same field. While it might seem to take a while to get his equipment properly positioned, it would make his efforts much more efficient once he got going.

He had parked the combine in a field about two miles from his farm. Brendon was rubbing his sore arm as he walked along the road and nodded at the drivers in the cars that passed him. A Washington County Sheriff's office SUV drove past and then braked hard. Brendon turned when he realized the vehicle was backing up next to him. The officer rolled down the window.

Brendon smiled and said, "Good morning, officer."

"Same to you. I couldn't help but notice your arm. It's all bloody, and what is that, duct tape?"

"Yes, sir. It's all I had in the toolbox."

"How did you hurt your arm?"

"I was working on the combine and slipped. My arm caught on a sharp edge."

"Was anyone else involved?"

"No, sir."

"How long ago did this happen?"

"Oh, I don't know. Two, maybe three hours ago."

"And it's still bleeding like that?"

"I guess so."

"You need to have someone look at that. Would you like me to call and get an ambulance out here for you?"

"I don't think that's necessary."

The conversation with the officer continued for another five minutes. Brendon assured the policeman he would immediately stop working and get attention for the wound. He phoned his doctor's office and was directed to go to the treatment facility on Medical Campus Road. Hopping into his truck, he first sent a text to Taylor, asking his sister to pick up Megan.

"Great. I can guess what I'll be doing all afternoon," Brendon grumbled as he fired up the truck. "Not how I wanted to spend my day." He'd been looking forward to seeing the expression on Megan's face when she walked out of school. Would she be happy or upset about him sending her flowers? He smiled and guessed that by now, the entire school had heard the news.

"It will just make it that much harder for you to back out of our engagement, honey."

The grin on his face departed as he considered what life would be like if she returned to London. There was only one thing to do.

"I need your help in this, Lord. If Megan feels I'm forcing her into this and it's not Your will, close the door firmly. But if us coming together is in Your master plan, help me find a solution to make Megan realize how I feel, and that not only do I need her, but I want to share my life with her as well. Please open Megan's eyes and help her come to the understanding that our engagement doesn't have to be pretend."

***

The school day was finally over. Megan waved goodbye to the last of the walkers and then collected her things. She paused for a few seconds to take in the sweet fragrance of the roses. Of course, her mind drifted to Brendon. He was such a sweet man and she wished it were all true. But nothing had changed the fact that she was heading back across the pond soon where her destiny, however bleak, waited for her.

Megan sighed as she straightened up the classroom. *Why did he have to send these roses?* Had it been Brendon's goal to embarrass her? *If so, he succeeded.*

Another thought raised its hand in her brain. *What if Brendon is serious about wanting me to be his fiancée and this isn't at all pretend to him?* As she swirled the thought around in her mind, Angie Levitt's question came back to her. *How old is Brendon?* Taylor was eight years senior to Megan and he was her older brother, but what was the age gap? Suppose he was two years Taylor's senior? That would make him thirty-seven to Megan's twenty-seven years. Would that be too great of a barrier to overcome?

"Oh, well. It's all make-believe, anyway." Megan grabbed her wrap and headed for the parking lot. She decided to be cross at him because, since all the other teachers knew, her work life was going to be a bit more difficult.

Megan had to shade her eyes against the bright sunshine. Brendon was usually parked in the same spot at the edge of the lot, but his truck was missing. She slowed, swiveling her head, but he wasn't in sight.

"Great," she muttered, "That will be something else for the busybodies to gossip about." Megan was just about to extract the mobile from her purse when she noted a baby blue and white vehicle quickly turn in. It was a Bronco—just like Taylor's. *Why would Taylor be here instead of Brendon?*

The Ford skidded to a stop right in front of her. Taylor had a worried look on her face. Megan opened the door.

"Hi. Why are you here instead of Brendon?"

"There's been an accident and that's all I know." Taylor shoved her phone into Megan's hands. "We're going to the emergency room now."

Tears filled her eyes as she tried to read Brendon's text.

Hey sis. Had a mishap. The sheriff's deputy told me I needed emergency treatment, so I'm headed to the Medical Center where I took you years ago when you broke your finger. Please pick up Megan for me and tell her I'm sorry. I really wanted to see the reaction on her face, but I guess I never will. Thanks, Bren

"What's he mean, 'I guess I never will'?" Megan asked as her voice rose. "Is he that ill or hurt that I can't see him again? Does that mean he doesn't want to see me or that he's afraid he won't make it?"

"I don't know. My brother rarely exaggerates about his injuries. When he got shot in Afghanistan, he told us he had a puncture wound. We didn't find out the extent of it until he returned home."

God, I know You're everywhere. Please watch over Brendon and heal him. Guide the hands of the doctors as they care for him. Megan found Taylor was watching her from time to time as they headed toward Hagerstown.

"Are you okay, Meg?"

"I'm just worried about your brother."

"Yeah, me too. The part about the sheriff's deputy has me concerned. I wonder if he had an accident with his truck."

"As long as he's okay, that's all I care about."

Another mile passed before Taylor spoke again. "What's in the long box?"

Heat ran up Megan's neck. "Roses—yellow ones."

"They're your favorite flower, right?"

"Yes."

"You got them at school?" Megan nodded. She didn't wish to have this conversation.

"Who are they from?"

"I'll give you one guess."

Taylor was silent for a moment. "Was it my brother?"

"Bingo."

Luckily, the medical facility loomed in front of them and Taylor didn't follow up with other inquiries.

The two women all but ran into the waiting area. Taylor approached the desk and asked about Brendon.

"He's in treatment," answered a receptionist old enough to be Megan's grandmother.

"Can I go see him?"

"Only family members are allowed beyond the waiting room."

"I'm his sister."

"Let me get someone to take you back." The older woman looked at Megan. "Are you family as well?"

"I'm his friend."

"Then have a seat. You can't go back there."

"She's more than his friend," Taylor replied quickly. "This is Megan McKenzie, my brother's fiancée."

Chapter Twenty-two

The medical staff grilled Megan even harder than her fellow teachers had about being Brendon's fiancée because she wasn't wearing an engagement ring. In the end, they were convinced enough to allow her to go back.

She and Taylor stood side by side when the nurse pulled back the curtain. Megan held her hand over her mouth as she caught a glimpse of Brendon. Her strong, lively fake fiancé was usually ready to tackle the world, but not today. He appeared to be sleeping as an IV dripped some sort of fluid into his right arm. The mid-part of his left arm was covered with a bandage and he sported a cast over his wrist.

Taylor touched his right hand. "Brendon, are you awake?" When he didn't answer the first time, his sister shook him firmly and called his name a bit louder.

"Okay, okay, I'm up. Geez, what's a guy got to do to get a nap around here?"

"What happened to you?" Taylor asked.

The man's eyes seemed confused. "Did you get my message about picking up Megan?"

"Of course."

"Where is she?"

"I'm here, Brendon." Megan stepped into his field of vision. The injured man's face lit up.

"I was worried you'd come out and no one would be there."

"She was fine," Taylor interjected, seemingly cross. "I picked her up. Now what happened to you?"

"Nothing major. I was greasing bearings on the corn head when I slipped."

"I see the bandages and, is that a cast?"

"Just a little one."

"How badly did you hurt yourself," Taylor seemed increasingly angry, "this time?"

"Well," Brendon replied as he scooted up in the bed, "nothing a bunch of stitches and some plaster couldn't fix."

Megan touched his arm and the man immediately took her hand. His gaze now drew Megan in.

"Did you break your arm?"

"Sort of. I fractured the ulnar bone right below the wrist. Nothing serious. You know me—a little bit of duct tape and a glass of milk and I'm good as new."

"Uh-huh," Taylor replied. "I see right through you. You were looking for a little time off, weren't you? All you had to do was ask. I could have collected eggs and fed the cows if you wanted help." Taylor shifted position. "Your note mentioned the deputy sheriff. Did you wreck the truck?"

"Of course not." Brendon took a few moments to explain the events leading up to his arrival at the medical center. Megan couldn't help but notice the way he gripped her hand. It was plain that Taylor saw it as well. Megan comprehended the expression on Taylor's face.

She's wondering why we're holding hands if everything is fake. What Taylor didn't understand was how quickly the depth of friendship had developed between Megan and Brendon. Taylor's brother had already replaced Taylor as Megan's best friend.

Is that the real reason our fingers are intertwined? Okay, if she was truly honest with herself, she was holding his hand out of relief. How would she have reacted if Brendon had been seriously hurt or worse? *I can't go there.* The time would come when Brendon would no longer be with her. *I'll worry about that then, but not while he's by my side.* For right now, there was no place she'd rather be than standing next to him and holding his hand.

The doctor came in and told Brendon he could leave as soon as the nurse disconnected his IV and reviewed the discharge instructions. The three of them were conferring about where to get supper when a commotion began on the other side of the curtain. A lively discussion was going on between a child and two adults.

"I'm sorry, ma'am. This is a hospital, not a daycare. Your daughter cannot stay here. Is there someone you would like me to call?" The authoritarian voice obviously belonged to a staff employee.

A worn-out voice replied, "There is no one else. It's just my daughter and me. If she can't stay here, what will happen? Where will she go?"

"We'll have to call Child Services. They'll make arrangements for your girl."

"Do you mean like sending her to a foster home?"

"I have no clue. What I do know is that they will act in the best interests of your daughter—who *cannot* stay here."

"I don't want to go, Mommy," cried a young girl.

Wait! I know that voice. Megan released Brendon's hand and walked to the curtain. Without hesitation, she threw the covering aside.

The small child turned at the action and her face lit up. The girl launched herself at Megan. "Ms. McKenzie! Why are you here?"

"I'm here with a friend." She held the child tightly. Without a second thought, Megan addressed the frail woman on the hospital bed. "I'm Megan McKenzie, your daughter's teacher. How can I be of assistance to you two?"

***

"Good morning, Chloe," Brendon said with a grin. "What do you want for breakfast—bacon and eggs or pancakes?"

"Pancakes," the little girl replied with a huge smile.

"Are pancakes all right with you two ladies?"

"Can you put blueberries in them?" Taylor asked.

"Sure. Special requests, Megan?"

"Not for the food, but would you mind making a cup of coffee for me? It was a late night." She stopped in her tracks. "Wait. Your arm is broken. Maybe I should do the cooking."

"I'm fine. I'm thinking the bones probably knitted back together already."

"Are you sure?"

"Of course. You must be tired after last night."

It had been a late evening for both women. After they were certain Brendon could safely drive home, the two friends had taken Chloe out to eat and then went shopping for 'essentials'. They came home with five or so large bags of clothing, toys and who knows what else for the little girl. He was so proud of Megan for how she always went out of her way to assist others.

It wasn't long before he moved a heaping pile of steaming blueberry pancakes and a platter of bacon to the table. Chloe's eyes bulged at the food before her.

While Megan filled the child's plate, Brendon grabbed the syrup, butter, powdered sugar, chocolate chips, rainbow sprinkles and whipped cream. Again, the child couldn't seem to remove her eyes from the items as he placed them on the table.

"Are we having a party?"

"Kind of," Megan replied to the girl. "We're celebrating you coming to stay with us for a while." She glanced at Brendon and Taylor. "Would you mind if I said prayers this morning?"

Both nodded for her to continue.

Megan took Chloe's hand. Brendon, sitting across the table, offered his to the girl. Chloe stared at him.

"Why are we holding hands?"

"We do this every time when we pray to God and thank Him for our blessings. It's our way of joining together when we talk to God. Is that okay?"

"Sure," Chloe responded timidly, but Brendon thought maybe the child was confused by this action.

"Good morning, Father. We wanted to thank You for this meal and the people sitting around the table. We ask You to watch over us and always keep us close. Thank You for protecting Brendon yesterday when he got hurt and for allowing Chloe to spend time with us. Help her grow in every way. Please keep watch on her mother, Jennifer, and heal her quickly so she and Chloe can be together again. In Your name we pray. Amen."

Chloe stared at Megan after she released her hand.

"Is something the matter?"

"Can we eat now?"

"Of course. Would you like any toppings?"

Megan asked Chloe which ones she wanted on her pancakes. Brendon chuckled to himself when Chloe said yes to all of them. He watched as the thin little girl ate as if she hadn't had food in months. After three helpings, she was finally full.

Megan and Taylor kept a good conversation going about the upcoming holidays. Chloe seemed a bit sad and when Taylor asked her why, the child told them she and her mother didn't celebrate any holidays or go to church.

"Anybody here still hungry?" he asked. All three shook their heads. Megan told Chloe to go brush her teeth and the girl departed. An air of sadness filled the room.

"When I see or hear about situations like this one," Taylor said, "I feel honored to have all the blessings we do. But part of my heart goes out to children like Chloe, who don't always get enough to eat."

"Mine, too," Megan added. "It makes me want to help them. At least in this case, we can. Did you hear what Chloe said—that she and her mother don't celebrate holidays or go to church?"

"Is that because her mother is sick?" Brendon asked.

"I'm not sure."

Taylor stirred her tea. "What's wrong with her mother?"

"Jennifer told me she has an immunity deficiency. Where our bodies might be able to fend off a cold quickly, the lady told me her body can't do that anymore."

"That would be hard on anyone," Taylor added, "especially when you're raising a child."

The conversation paused briefly. Brendon studied Megan and saw, or thought he saw, two things. He was beginning to know her well enough to read her moods and sometimes even her mind. She was definitely sad, but then he picked up on the other thing—determination. He suspected Megan was prepared to go above and beyond to assist Chloe. His heart burst with pride for the young Brit's tenacity.

"What can I do to help?" he asked.

Without hesitation, Megan replied, "Chloe will get out of school half an hour before I leave. Would you mind picking her up?"

"Of course not."

"Thank you," Megan replied as she started to clean off the table.

"Know why I agreed so quickly?" He caught not only the questioning look Megan sent his way, but the smile on Taylor's lips as she watched the exchange.

"Enlighten me."

"It's practice."

"Practice for what?"

"When we have kids." While Megan's face turned bright red, Taylor started giggling.

"I beg your pardon?"

"You know—kids, children, babies. Like ours. And just so you know—I want at least eight. How many would you like, honey?"

Taylor burst out in a belly laugh.

Megan shot his sister a nasty look. "Eight children? Are you out of your mind?"

"Yep." Brendon blew a kiss in her direction. "Out of my mind in love with you—like any fiancé would be."

All the color had now drained from her face. She walked over and stood face to face with him. Megan's voice was but a whisper. "Are you being serious?"

"About what?" Brendon asked as he took his plate to the sink, then grabbed his jacket and headed for the door. "Having that many kids?"

She followed him. "N-no. About the other thing you said."

"What do you think... *honey*?" He sent a wink her way before heading outside to start his day.

Chapter Twenty-three

"*I*'ve never been to a church. What do they do inside?" Chloe was in the rear seat of Brendon's truck as they drove to the Sunday service.

Megan spun around and glanced at her charge. "We come here to worship God."

"But Mr. Brendon told me God is everywhere. Why do we go here if He's all around?"

Megan knew Brendon had a long talk with Chloe about God and who He was. Chloe told him that was the first time anyone had told her about God or Jesus.

"Well, what Brendon said is entirely true." She glanced at the man who was driving for assistance in answering. He blew her a kiss. *What? I need your help and all you want to do is flirt—go figure!*

"The purpose of going to church," Brendon suddenly interjected, "is so we can hang out with others who love God. People call this fellowship. When we get to Heaven, there will be lots of people who believe in God, so we take time to be with them now." He winked at Megan. "A good friend of mine once told me church is like going to a hospital."

"Like where my mommy is staying?"

"In a sense, yes. Going here can make us get better at loving God."

After a pause, Chloe asked, "Will we see Mommy today?"

"We were planning to visit her this afternoon," Megan stated. "Would you like that?"

"Uh-huh. I like your house, but I really miss my mommy. I wish we could live with you. I like the cows and chickens. It's fun picking eggs. And I love Orville. I've never had a dog to play with before."

Megan glanced at Brendon. The smile from earlier was gone. She imagined allowing Jennifer and Chloe to move in might be too much—especially because Megan's time to stay with Brendon and Taylor was drawing to a close.

"It looks packed today," Brendon commented as he turned into the church lot. "I don't see either Chuck or Taylor's vehicles, do you?"

"No. Taylor told me they were going to breakfast with his parents. Maybe they're running late or decided to skip today."

He found a spot for his Ford and the three of them walked inside. Chloe was between them, holding both of their hands. They found Pastor Rollins at the door to the sanctuary, shaking hands. His face broke into a wide smile when he caught sight of them.

"Well, look who it is—the lovebirds." He bent down and reached for Chloe's hand. "And how are you, young lady?

Chloe turned away and hid her face in Megan's skirt.

"This is Chloe," Megan replied. "She's just a tad shy."

"Is this your little girl?"

Megan felt her face heat. "No. She's the daughter of a friend. Chloe's staying with us for a while."

"Well, we're glad to have you with us." The pastor turned to the next couple in line as the trio entered the sanctuary.

"Where would you like to sit... Mommy?" If possible, Brendon's comment made her cheeks even warmer than before.

"How about front and center, *Pops?* That way you can keep an eye on your friend."

Chloe was wide-eyed as the service began. The choir processed and when the singers sat in the loft directly in front of them, Chloe partially hid herself in Megan's skirt. And, as Megan expected, Trina Lewis stared down on them from less than thirty feet away. There appeared to be something different about the woman today. Her smile was radiant.

After the processional hymn finished, she looked directly at Megan and mouthed, "Good morning." Megan returned the gesture with a nod.

Pastor Rollins highlighted some of the printed announcements from the bulletin.

"As Thanksgiving approaches, please remember our shut-ins. We would like to deliver baskets of good cheer. You'll find the donation list of items needed inside the bulletin. Where we need help is not only the canned food list, but for delivery drivers who are willing to drop off the baskets and spend a few minutes brightening the day of people who can't get out anymore. Please see Trina Lewis if you'd like to volunteer."

It felt as if someone shook her shoulder, but Megan knew if she turned, there would be no one there. She imagined it was the hand of God. Megan reached over Chloe and tapped Brendon's arm. He shot her a smile.

"Can I sign us up to do this?"

"Of course, honey. We can take Chloe along, if you'd like."

Megan knew her face was beaming as she turned from him. Trina's stare drew Megan's attention. The lady with the perfect hair mouthed to Megan, "Are you going to help?" Megan nodded and was rewarded with a gigantic smile. Megan believed the gesture was genuine.

"And finally, as the Christmas season approaches, seven of the local churches will once again be participating in the Hemlock Trail. For those of you unfamiliar with this local tradition, the Hemlock Trail is a collection of homes and churches that are decorated for the Christmas season. We had about three hundred people visit the sixteen sites last year." He paused and looked out over the congregation.

"Those who know me well might recall the friendly rivalry between myself and my very good friend, Jim Chilcoat. Jim is the pastor of Good Samaritan in Smithsburg. Each year, he and I make a little wager over which of our churches will have the most participants. Well, he beat me last December for the fifth year in a row. I sure would like to get the best of my buddy, but I can't do it without your help. Do I have any volunteers?"

To Megan's utter disbelief, Brendon stood.

"Brendon Davis," Pastor Rollins said. "Would you like to participate?"

Brendon reached for Megan's hand and whispered, "Just go with it. I'll explain later." With trembling knees, she stood. Chloe did as well. Brendon winked at both of them.

"Well, Pastor Rollins, as some here in the congregation might have heard, I'm going to marry this young lady, Megan McKenzie, sometime in the near future." Brendon paused and everyone in the congregation clapped and cheered. Her face heated to a level that would melt tool steel. Once again, Brendon sent a smile her way before continuing.

"Meg and I would love to share our home with those who travel the Hemlock Trail." He paused and looked directly at her. "Is that all right with you, Meg?"

What could she do? Forcing a smile, she nodded her head.

"That settles it," Pastor Rollins commented. "The future Mr. and Mrs. Davis are the first volunteers to represent our church. Anyone else want to sign up?" Surprisingly, two other couples stood up and volunteered.

After they sat back down, Megan couldn't help but stare at Brendon. Was the man crazy or simply out of his mind? The words he'd muttered just days ago came back to her. She thought at the time he was teasing, but now, Megan wasn't certain.

"I'm out of my mind in love with you."

He did realize the engagement was fake, didn't he? And he knew Megan had said what she did only to protect him from Trina. Or was there more here than meets the eye? Brendon knew absolutely nothing about the will, so it couldn't be about the money. A sudden revelation filled her mind. Could it be that, for the first time in her life, there was really a man who was truly and utterly in love with her?

Chapter Twenty-four

After church, Brendon drove them back to the farm. He'd gotten up early and placed a roast in the slow cooker. When they turned into the drive, Megan pointed out that Chuck's Charger was parked out front.

"Looks like my sister and future brother-in-law were playing hooky. We might just want to have a talk with them about that."

"There's something I wish to discuss with you, as well... later, when we're alone." He glanced at Megan, who motioned that Chloe was seated in the back.

I can read you like a book, honey. Megan wanted to find out why Brendon had let everyone know about the 'fake' engagement. She also wished to discuss the Hemlock Trail event, which he'd volunteered both of them for.

"Okay, honey."

They had barely climbed out of the truck when Taylor appeared on the porch. Despite the chill in the air, she wasn't wearing a coat.

"You know," Brendon said as he prepared to tease his sister, "sick people should bundle up when it's cold outside."

Taylor walked to him and, despite the frown, he knew a smile was ready to burst onto her face. She placed the back of her hand on his forehead.

"What are you doing?"

"I thought you might have a fever."

"Why would you think I did? You were the one who wasn't well enough to attend church."

"Oh, we were there, but you didn't see us."

"You were? Where?"

"The service had started, so we snuck in the back and sat in the next to last pew."

"Ms. McKenzie," asked Chloe, "could you help me pick out a dress to wear when we visit Mommy?"

"I bought you three dresses, sweetie. Just pick out whichever one you would fancy to wear this afternoon."

"But I really want you to help me decide."

Megan's eyes met Brendon's and he knew immediately that his fake fiancée wanted to talk—like now, if not sooner.

"After you help Chloe, maybe you could give me a hand finishing the lunch preparations?"

"I'd be *delighted*." Megan's inflection told him that wasn't what she meant. Brendon had some explaining to do and Megan couldn't wait.

"I'll be in momentarily."

"Okay-y-y," she said, dragging out the word. It was becoming plain Megan wanted answers.

He began to head for the front door, but Taylor grabbed his arm.

"Did you want something?"

"Brother, are you feeling well?"

"Of course."

"Are you drunk?"

"You know I don't drink."

"Then can you explain what came over you today?"

"What do you mean?"

"You told the entire congregation you were going to marry Megan."

"Yes, I did."

"Why did you lie to them?"

He sensed the smile on his lips. "Why do you think I was lying?"

"You know it's fake, right?"

"That's what Megan says."

"Then why did you..." Taylor's hands covered her mouth. "Jumping Jehosaphat! You're in love with her, aren't you?"

"As a matter of fact, I am."

"But still you know this isn't real, don't you?"

"Taylor, I love Megan, and inside, I know she feels the same. She just won't admit it—yet. She can pretend all she wants that this is a scam, but I'm going to make it plain as the nose on her pretty face—she and I belong together."

"Megan is heading back to London next month."

"She may think that, but I'm going to open her eyes and change her mind. Megan and I were meant to be. I won't give up until she realizes it, too."

"Is that why you volunteered for the Hemlock Trail?"

"Of course. Together we can decorate the house, prepare the food and then jointly host the event. It will be fun—like a team-building exercise so she can see first-hand how great of a couple we are. Not only will it draw us together, she'll have the time of her life. After it's over, I'll suggest we do it every year and I know she'll agree. It's a fail-proof plan."

Taylor's expression sobered. "Suppose she still wants to go home?"

"Sis, I truly believe God brought us together. We fit together even better than Noelle and I did. I believe it is His master plan that brought her here."

"But suppose—"

"In Philippians it says *'I can do all things through Jesus'*. With His help, I'll succeed."

"And what if you're completely wrong and it isn't in His plan for you two to be together?"

"Then I'll suffer the consequences. But I really believe He destined Megan for me and me for her. And I'm going to do everything in my power not only to follow God's will, but to convince Megan as well." Brendon could tell by Taylor's expression that she had her doubts.

"Come on, Taylor. Just trust me. After all, I'm your older and wiser big brother."

She shook her head. "Yeah. Keep telling yourself that."

Chapter Twenty-five

*M*egan had hurriedly assisted Chloe. The little girl was getting ready as Megan bolted down the stairs. She found Brendon in the kitchen putting together the instant mashed potatoes.

"There you are. We need to talk."

He raised his eyebrows as he shot her a smile. "Yes, honey?"

"What in God's name were you thinking?"

"How pretty my fiancée is."

"Stop it." Her cheeks warmed because once again, the man was flirting with her. "You know precisely what I'm speaking about."

"I do?"

"Why did you tell everyone we were engaged?"

He looked confused. "Wait. You said it first. I was just repeating what you told Trina."

"In private!"

"And she told everyone else. You know, there was something strange going on at church. Maybe I'm mistaken, but it appeared the two of you were having a quiet conversation."

"Don't change the subject on me. Why did you do that?"

"I was simply playing along."

"No, you weren't. You were inflating my lie."

"You started it."

"Uhm," she huffed in frustration. "This will backfire on you. When I go back to London, everyone will think you're a grand fool and I'm horrible. Or was that your point? Are you trying to build me up as the villain?"

His eyes softened and his expression made her heart skip a beat. "I would never do that, Megan. I think the world of you, maybe even more than you know."

"You do understand I only did this in a moment of weakness to try and protect you from her?"

"Can I ask you a question?"

"Do I have a choice?"

Brendon seemed to ignore her response.

"Can you pretend for a moment that it's real?"

"There's nothing I'd like more, but face the truth, Brendon—it's not."

"Can you at least pretend? Wasn't that what you asked me to do?"

"Yes, but—"

"Then, it's settled. Let's act like we're two people who are madly in love. Would that be so bad?"

"Brendon, in the end you will just be hurt by having people believe we're going to be married."

He offered a smile. "With all due respect, you've already sent that ship to sea. I think you know me well enough by now to understand that when I do something, I commit—totally."

"In other words, you want everybody to believe this falsehood."

"I want everyone to believe what you said."

"Might I ask why?"

"If you don't know by now, you will soon."

Megan was beyond confused. "I don't understand you at all."

"You will in time. Just remember—you started this. Now, we have something urgent to discuss."

"What could be more important than us?" *Wait, did I really say that?*

"Nothing, but time is of the essence."

"I'm totally baffled."

"It's fine, we'll work through it together."

"What in Heaven's name are you talking about?"

"The Hemlock Trail. We have five weeks to transform this old farmhouse into a Christmas fantasy land—one *Better Homes and Gardens* would feature on their cover."

"I beg your pardon?"

"People will come from far and wide to see our place—and what you and I have done to decorate it. Then, there's the menu to consider."

"What menu?"

"Honey, you and I are hosting people in our home. That's the purpose of the Hemlock Trail. It's a sort of progressive dinner. After church, I told Pastor Rollins we would provide the dessert course."

"For how many people?"

"Who knows? The pastor said about three hundred people came last year. I think we should prepare food for four hundred."

"You are out of your mind. Four hundred people? That's a lot of food."

"Don't worry. Whatever is left over we'll donate to the soup kitchen."

"What are you planning to make?"

"That's the best part," he snickered.

"Come again?"

"You and I will decide and prepare it together. Side by side in the kitchen," he paused and winked at her, "just like two old married people would do."

Chapter Twenty-six

"Why did I volunteer to do this if you aren't helping me?"

Brendon shook his head as he glanced from behind the wheel. "We didn't talk about it first. Daylight hours are getting shorter and shorter and I still have lots of acres of corn to harvest. I'm sorry I can't help you deliver food to shut-ins today." He hesitated and Megan detected a smile forming on his lips. "But there is a bright side. It might be a lot of fun, meeting new people—you know, while helping others."

"Really? Is that what you truly believe, since you obviously find my predicament humorous?"

"A recap of recent history would reveal you speak sometimes without thoroughly thinking through the ramifications. Take for example your confession to Trina—you know, where you revealed the true desire of your heart by saying we were engaged."

"You love to make fun of me and my errors, don't you?"

They had arrived at the church. A handful of cars were there. Thankfully, Megan didn't see Trina's Mercedes.

"You only pick on the ones you love." The tone of Brendon's voice made her turn her head to see his eyes.

What she had at first dismissed as her imagination was starting to reveal itself every time they spoke. Megan was now convinced the man was undeniably in love with her. Something caught in her chest. Brendon was the man she'd dreamed about when she was younger, before the reading of her grandmother's will. *If things were different, I would be on cloud nine.*

"It's all pretend, Brendon," she whispered. *Okay, maybe not everything.*

"Whatever you say, honey." He softly took her hand and raised it to his lips. "No, wait. Open your eyes and your heart, Megan." Brendon's voice had never been as clear. "Quit kidding yourself. Take a good look at what's in front of you, then tell me it's only make-believe for you."

It was getting harder and harder to keep up the façade—not just for everyone else to see, but the truth between them. If she was totally honest with herself... *No! Stop this.*

"Don't do this to me when you're about to leave. Maybe a nasty, public breakup of our fictitious engagement would get your attention?"

He recoiled and dropped her hand. "Well, okay then. I am certainly sorry. What time would you like to be picked up?"

Great. Now he looked wounded, hurt, and victimized. Thinking about Brendon's sad mood would undoubtedly ruin her evening. "I didn't mean to burst your bubble. It's just..." Her voice faded because she didn't know how to say what she needed to. "May I call you to come collect me when I'm finished?"

He looked away. "I, uh, on second thought—call Taylor. I'm going to go pick corn. The weatherman is calling for rain or snow early next week, then with Thanksgiving coming up... I need to get the crop harvested. I'm way behind."

Now he wants to act like a scolded child? "If that's what you want...*fine!* I'll ring her afterwards."

"Tremendous. I'll probably be on the combine until late, so I'll bid you a good night now."

"You as well." Megan stepped from the truck and slammed the door. *That man infuriates me!*

He at least waited until she was at the door before driving off. *I hate it when we fight right before he leaves.*

Okay, this was probably their first quarrel, but still. How could this farmer make her so angry?

A voice inside her spoke out. *Hold onto this anger. It will make it easier to cope when you leave him behind.*

Megan needed to think that one over. While returning to London had never been appealing, the thought of life without Brendon was becoming almost unbearable to consider.

Wait! Would I be willing to give up everything for a chance at a future with Brendon? A great thought, but there was no guarantee they could get it right. Most likely, at some point in the future, his eyes would be opened and he would come to the realization Megan was nothing special. When that happened, she would lose everything.

Before she could continue with her mind's soliloquy, a voice rang out.

"Megan, it's good to see you. How are you tonight?"

Great. On top of everything else—Trina Lewis is here. Megan forced a smile.

"Oh, I'm fine, just fine." This was the first time she'd caught a glimpse of Trina without the choir robe. Her nemesis wore designer jeans and a printed top. Her clothes were tasteful, yet failed to hide the woman's perfect figure. Combine that with her pretty face and perfectly styled hair, how could any girl ever compete with this woman? No wonder Brendon turned to putty at her touch.

"All of the goodies have been divided out. There are six shut-in itineraries for tonight and five of the routes have couples slated for delivering. What do you think? Would you like to join me?"

Not if I have a choice. "Sure. How can I help?"

"I borrowed an Escalade from Daddy's Cadillac dealership, so there will be plenty of room for the supplies. How about giving me a hand loading up? All the boxes are in the kitchen. I'll bring the Caddy around—just meet me there, okay?"

"Sure, but could you point me in the direction of the kitchen?"

Trina laughed and then showed Megan the way so she wouldn't get lost.

It would be a few minutes before the other woman arrived. Megan yanked her cell from her jeans and opened the texting app. Of course, numerous messages from George the fourth were waiting. She ignored them as the hurt look on

Brendon's face from earlier replayed itself in her mind.

Our first real beef happens just before he leaves. Her snarky comment about a nasty breakup sounded like a great jab, until she realized she'd actually hurt Brendon's feelings. *What should I do?*

Megan's fingers seemed to have their own opinion and within a few seconds, had created a message:

> Brendon, so sorry for what I said. I don't want a breakup of either our fake engagement or (especially) our friendship. Let's talk when I get back and make things better, all right?

"Everything okay?"

With what she was sure was a deer in the headlight expression, Megan shoved the device back into her pocket and faced Trina.

"I'm quite good."

Trina nodded in the direction of Megan's cell. "I hate those things. Why can't people just talk face to face, you know?"

"That I do."

Within minutes, all the supplies were loaded into the monstrous SUV, which reminded Megan of a rail car—make that a luxury one at that.

"Our first stop is Janie Dempsey's place. Poor lady lost her husband two years ago."

"I bet that puts her in a bit of a pickle."

"What?" Trina asked with a laugh. "I love the way you talk."

"I meant it must be rough on her."

"Yes, it is. Can I say something?"

Oh great! Here we go. "Of course."

"I'm really glad I met you, but I'm even happier Brendon found you."

"Come again?"

"I know I came on a bit strong a while back, but I didn't lie to you."

"About?"

"Wanting the best for Brendon. I do love him and always will, but seeing how happy he is when he's with you, it just makes my heart jump for joy."

How do I answer that?

"Thanks."

"I remember the first time I saw him, I mean *really* saw him as he is."

Megan remained silent.

"It was when he was with Noelle. In those days, I believed the world was like a fruit, ready to be plucked. And I picked him." Trina's sniff surprised Megan. "I messed up life for him, well, both of them."

"He told me about what happened with Noelle. Brendon really loved her."

"He did and I was the idiot who came between them. It seemed I had him wrapped around my finger and I loved that. But like the fool I am... I threw him away."

"Why?"

"A shinier object caught my attention. I know you said Brendon hadn't mentioned me, but I don't think that's quite true. I'm sure your fiancé told you about my repeated screw-ups. When I was younger, I believed I could have my cake and eat it, too."

"You've told me you loved Brendon. And yes, he mentioned to me how you cheated on him—repeatedly. How could you do that to someone you love?"

Trina released a loud sigh and ran her hand through her hair. "Because I was the world's biggest idiot. The final straw was what Brendon walked in on the last time we were together. My dad had told me Brendon asked for my hand in marriage and Dad agreed. I wanted one last fling before settling down. I never, in my wildest dreams, would have thought he'd catch me."

Megan noted the quick wipe of Trina's hand over her cheek.

"That was the worst night of my life. You can believe it or not, but I changed right then and there. I vowed to God I would be faithful to Brendon and also that I'd wait for him and him alone. I prayed your man would change his heart, forgive me and allow me one more chance."

Trina turned off the main road, following the GPS directions on the Caddy's information screen. "I imagine this seems like a strange conversation between us."

"Not to worry."

"There's a reason I'm sharing all this with you."

"Honestly, it doesn't matter."

"It does to me. You see, I made one more vow to God I didn't tell anyone about."

Megan noticed her hands were sweaty. "Okay?"

"I promised God that if He sent someone special to Brendon, that I'd... that I would allow myself to finally move on—to find someone else." Despite the tears on her cheek, Trina was smiling. "You're here, so that is what I've been waiting for—God's sign for me. You are the answer to my prayers—Brendon's true happiness." Trina drew a deep a breath. "Thank you for coming into not only Brendon's life, but mine as well."

"I am not following you."

"It's simple, Megan. Because of you, I finally get the chance to move on. Now, I can actually live my own life and find real happiness."

Chapter Twenty-seven

*G*etting out of bed had been a monumental struggle that morning. Of course, he'd only laid his head on the pillow three hours before. Brendon had spent last evening and the wee hours in the cab of the combine working through countless rows of field corn. Twice he'd filled up the grain trailer and then offloaded the crop into the silo.

Brendon poured a mug of coffee and removed the bread from the toaster. He slathered it with butter and raspberry jam.

Thoughts of Megan had consumed him last evening, even in his dreams. *Can she not see how much I love her?* Blurting out their false engagement, to no less than Trina Lewis, had seemed ridiculous at the time. But after closely examining his soul, Brendon realized Megan was everything he'd ever dreamed of—his heart's greatest desire. He wanted it all to be real, to share every second of his life with her, but there was one problem. That wasn't what she wanted. In silence, he finished his toast.

"Is it that she can't see I love her, Lord, or is the thought of being stuck with me simply that revolting?"

Footfalls on the stairs drew his attention. Megan stumbled into the kitchen.

"Good morning," Brendon said as he greeted her with a smile.

"To you as well."

The expression on her face didn't agree with her words.

"Want me to make you some coffee?"

"I'm quite capable of preparing it myself, thank you." She slammed the coffee cup onto the counter and walked to the fridge to grab the creamer. "I know you have a busy schedule these days. Will you have time to drop Chloe off at school or should I ring for an Uber?"

"I'll do it." It seemed someone was in a foul mood this morning.

"I spoke to her mother last evening. Jennifer will be released today, so Chloe is going home. Just one less task to bother you with."

"She's not a bother," he hesitated before adding, "and neither are you."

She nodded, but failed to look in his direction.

"Your actions don't reflect your words."

"Now what did I do?"

After filling her cup, she spun to face him so quickly that coffee sloshed from her mug.

"You were in such a hurry to harvest your precious corn last night. Did you get it all picked?"

"No, but I made a sizeable dent in it."

"Your work kept you so busy you couldn't even answer my text. I can see I must not be important to you. Or is it that you received my message, but I wasn't significant enough for you to even reply?"

"I didn't get any messages from you last evening—text or voice. The only communication you gave me was the reminder that our engagement is phony."

The way the blue in Megan's eyes seemed to flare gave Brendon a warning. A full-blown hurricane was about to land on him.

"I most certainly did text you."

"No, you didn't."

"Did so."

"You can say it all you want, but I received nothing from you after I left."

The glare on her face indicated he was in for it. Removing his device, he tapped open the screen and offered it to Megan.

"If you don't believe me, look for yourself."

Megan ripped the cell from his hand and slipped her finger across the screen.

"What, did you delete it?"

"I'd have to get something first before discarding it."

Her scowl did little to hide Megan's true beauty. "Perhaps I dumped it by mistake. Check the trash folder."

Brendon took a long sip of coffee while Megan scrolled through his gadget. "Find what you're looking for?"

Her expression was less severe now—more confused than angry. Placing his phone on the counter, she looked at her device.

"I could have sworn I sent it." Suddenly, Megan's face turned bright pink. "Crap, here it is, still in draft." She closed her eyes and swallowed hard. "Sorry."

Realizing he could get mileage out of this if he played his cards right, Brendon quickly did the opposite. *After all, God wants us to forgive each other. What would I want Megan to do if this was me?*

"No worries, Meg. We're both here right now. Tell me what you were going to send and we can talk, face to face, in person."

Megan turned away. "It's not important anymore."

"You sure?" Something wasn't adding up correctly. Did she want to talk—or just find fault with him? This was a side of Megan he'd never seen before. "Two minutes ago you were ready to rip off my arm and beat me over the head with it because I didn't respond to your message. And now, we should just simply forget it?"

"As I indicated, the time to talk about the topic is past."

"And you no longer wish to discuss it?"

"That's correct."

"Well, great, that's just fine. Do you have anything else you want to not talk about before I begin my day?"

"No."

"Okay then." Brendon drained his cup and placed it on the sink. "I'm off to feed the animals. I'll be back in time to take both you and Chloe to school—unless you want Taylor to drop you off."

"It's up to *you*." She'd drawn out and emphasized the last word, making him aware she wanted a response.

"Then I'll take you—if you're up to it."

"And that wouldn't be an issue for the master farmer?"

"Of course not." He wanted to add, *I never mind spending time with you,* but that seemed to be the inappropriate word choice today.

"Fine, then."

Brendon was almost to the door when she spoke again.

"I take it you're not having breakfast with us?"

"That's correct. There's a lot on my to-do list today."

"Picking corn again, huh?"

"Later I will. This morning, I have to grind up feed for the cattle. That takes a couple of hours."

"Then don't tarry because of me."

"Like I told you before, you're never a bother to me, Meg." His words failed to evoke even a simple smile. "Bye for now, *honey*."

He was reaching for the knob when Megan again spoke.

"You'll never guess who my delivery partner was last evening, *darling*."

Brendon rolled his eyes and then put on a smiling face before turning to the young Brit.

"Please forgive me. I forgot to ask. How was your evening?"

"It was just peachy. Thank you for noticing my benevolent actions."

"That was kind of you. Did the shut-ins appreciate what you delivered?"

"I do believe our conversations were more important to them than the sustenance we dropped off."

Brendon sat down on a chair. He knew Megan had something she wanted to talk about, and his assignment, if he chose to accept it, was to figure out what it was... or more likely, how to coax it out of her.

"What time did you get home?"

"It was pushing ten."

"Whoa, it took six hours to deliver food to shut-ins? How did Taylor handle that, I mean, did she bring Chloe along? Had I known it was that late, I would have picked you up."

"You were too busy, remember? We were finished by six-thirty. And I made other arrangements to get back here so I didn't need to inconvenience either Taylor or Chloe... and especially not you."

"Really?"

"What?" Megan asked with an accusatory expression on her face. "Don't you think I can get along without you?"

"I never said that. Who gave you a lift?"

"My delivery partner." The smile on her face didn't add up because it obviously wasn't real. She was trying to make a point, but for the life of him, Brendon had no clue what it was.

"Who might that have been?"

"Your old girlfriend—Trina Lewis."

Chapter Twenty-eight

$\mathcal{M}$egan's response certainly got his attention. Brendon's face lost all color.

"You spent last evening with Trina? No wonder you're distraught. Was she mean to you?"

"First, I am not upset. Secondly, Trina and I had a wonderful time."

"What? Did I hear you correctly?" He moved closer to her. "After the way she hounded you the night you told her... well, you know what you said."

That you and I were engaged? "Trina was quite pleasant. She filled me in on her side of the equation between you."

"And let me guess, now I'm the villain?"

"Quite the opposite. Trina expressed sincere remorse for interfering with you and Noelle. Then she told me her account of how she lost you."

His hands trembled on the table. "I never anticipated her throwing that curve ball. Just what did she say to you?"

"That she was wrong for trying to have her cake and eat it, too."

"Cake? Would you please speak clearly? I hate games and this feels like one."

"With all due respect, you are wrong. I'm simply retelling Trina's version of the story."

"And what exactly was the point she was trying to make?"

She had to pause for a moment. Megan wanted to tell him the truth—that her bitterness this morning was directed more at herself than him. She knew exactly what would happen when she departed. Brendon would be sad and vulnerable. Trina would be there to soothe and comfort him. And in the end, Brendon would marry Trina because she was a better choice for him. *At least one of us should experience some form of love.* What was waiting for her in London would never be love—Megan would simply be the object of George's lust for money and domination.

"Are you okay? You look as if you might cry."

She rubbed her eyes furiously. "I am absolutely fine."

"What did the witch say to you to make you think like this?"

"Trina expressed to me just how happy she is because you found me and she feels free now. The lady told me she can finally move on."

"What? Wait. This isn't making any sense."

"Those were her words, but the thing is, I don't believe that's what she meant. Brendon, that woman is still deeply in love with you."

He stood and his face turned blood red. "I certainly *do not* feel the same, and I never will."

"If you really desire true love, you should get back together with Trina."

"Pigs will fly first. I'd rather become a hermit, sentenced to life in solitary confinement than spend one second of my life with her by my side."

"Face the facts—she loves you."

"Yet I don't feel the same. Don't you realize why?" Before Megan could give her input, Brendon continued. "I am in love with you, Megan. Can't you see that?"

They remained as they were for a few minutes— Megan sitting and Brendon looking down at her. He was breathing heavily. She touched his hand.

"You might think that, but you don't really mean it."

"How can you say that? Can't you see... or more importantly, *feel* the truth of my words?"

"It's only infatuation. One day you will grow tired of my accent and my face. There's not much we have in common. I mean, you're what, almost fifteen years older than I am? When I'm forty, you'll be fifty-five." She studied his face. "Trina is closer to your age."

He exhaled loudly. "The years we've lived are just a number. Let me tell you this, my friend. I can out work, out last and most importantly, show you a deeper and truer love than any man you'll ever meet."

I don't doubt that. You will always be the great love of my life. She struggled not to allow her emotions to surface. "My return to Great Britain will be best for both of us."

He sat across from her and gently took her hand. "I don't get this. Help me understand where you are coming from."

She was so close to dropping her shield and revealing everything. "Last night after we finished our deliveries, Trina and I visited Chloe's mother in the hospital. That's when Jennifer told me she will be discharged today."

"What does Chloe's mom have to do with us?"

"Jennifer made a series of bad choices when she was young and those regrets will most likely shorten her life." Despite the change in the topic, Brendon listened as she continued. "She can barely get by and the cost of her medications is outrageous."

"We have agencies in America who can assist her, both financially and emotionally."

"Though in different circumstances, I've been where she is. There never seemed to be enough of what we needed. I want to, no, I *will* make a difference in the lives of Chloe and Jennifer and others like them, people in need."

"You do understand that *we* can do that—together."

"I want to spend my life assisting others."

"I know that, and that's exactly what you are doing. That's precisely why Taylor became a teacher—to help others. Your compassion and empathy are making a difference—look at what you did for Chloe."

She had to make him understand.

"Do you believe in the greater good?"

"I'm not sure I follow you."

"Suppose you followed in the footsteps of the Lord? Would you be willing to sacrifice your happiness so others could experience joy?"

"The answer to that question doesn't have to be an 'either/or' choice. Do you think that you have to give up your own happiness to assist others? I hope you realize the two are not mutually exclusive. Besides, I think a person who experiences true enjoyment in their own life is better equipped to serve others. Don't you agree?"

Brendon was speaking directly to her heart. Internally, they were on the same page, but the fact remained—that pot of gold waiting on her would do so much good for so many. It was her chance to change the world.

"I'm sorry, Brendon. I'm committing my life to the service of others, not satisfying my own desires."

It was as if he'd just received news that every person he cared about had perished. Brendon clasped his hands together to cover his mouth and then looked away. His eyes were suddenly glossy.

"I must seem to be an utter fool to you. I completely misread you and your feelings. My apologies, Megan. We can skip the charade of the faux engagement. I'll cancel my participation in the Hemlock Trail."

"But you've already committed to it."

His expression did not change.

She touched his hand. "Let's do it together. It will still be fun—a great memory for both of us to cherish."

He slowly pushed her hand from his arm.

Brendon stood and then walked to the door. "Let me consider it. I need to get my day started. I'll be back in time to take both of you to school." He departed without another word.

Megan stood, watching until his profile disappeared from view.

"I am doing the right thing, aren't I, Lord?" Usually, she felt at least some warmth when she spoke with God. Today, there was nothing, until a text arrived. Hoping it would be from Brendon, she yanked the device from her pocket.

> Megan, great news. While you've been avoiding me, I booked our honeymoon. We depart New Year's Day from London on a private yacht, bound for our four-month tour of the Mediterranean and Africa. I've spared no expense in booking this trip. Call me so I can tell you about the wedding (and honeymoon) details I've planned. Your husband-to-be, George (but you can call me your sweet G4)

"I bet you spared no possible expense—using my grandmother's money."

The thought of marrying this evil man turned her stomach—literally. She barely made it to the water closet. As she knelt before the toilet, she thought she heard a voice.

"Are you happy with your plans to serve Me?" Turning quickly, she expected to find the owner of the voice, but there was no one there.

Could the words have come from God? If so, what did they mean?

Chapter Twenty-nine

While mixing the food for the cattle, Brendon made the decision to go through with the commitment to host the Hemlock Trail. At first, he convinced himself it was the perfect way to show both Trina and Megan he would be fine. After all, he was a survivor. When Megan left, he would display a 'who cares' attitude. Public opinion would cast Megan as wrong for turning her back on the life Brendon could provide her. And the whole county would see her for exactly what she was—a narrow-minded fool!

Do you really believe that?

Brendon was surprised his heart was challenging his mind. Why would his heart defend her when she was the one who was breaking it in two?

She wants to devote her life to helping others. Who are you to stand in her way, holding Megan back from her destiny? He hadn't thought of it that way. All he had considered were his own feelings.

Do you actually love Megan or is it the feeling of being in love?

Of course he loved her, with all his heart.

If that's true, quit harassing the girl. Instead, do your best to support her.

Brendon chewed that one over in his mind. Megan might not love him in the same manner he loved her, but love her he did. She was the most significant person in his entire life. Instead of acting angry or hurt, why couldn't he instead do his best to encourage her? Maybe show his friendship through his actions, not by hurtful words.

Once his heart convinced his mind, the decision about what to do next was easy. She only had a few weeks left before going home. Brendon was going to give her happy memories to treasure for a lifetime. It all became clear—in fact, it seemed as if a great weight had been lifted from him. He could show his true self in their friendship and not worry about what was real versus fake.

He hurried back to the house and flung open the door. Chloe was sitting at the table eating. Megan and Taylor stood at the counter near the coffee maker.

"Morning, everyone. Megan, would you mind stepping outside with me for a moment?"

He could see that was the last thing she wanted to do, but she followed him without a word. There was a chill in the air and he sensed she minded it.

Megan opened the discussion. "I don't want another argument. What do you have to say?"

He yanked off his jacket and quickly draped it over her shoulders. "I thought about what you said and I owe you a gigantic apology. You mean so much to me. If it's okay with you, I'd like to continue our friendship as it was before all this happened. Like you said earlier, we still have the chance to make memories—good ones we can each cherish—forever."

Megan's expression had not changed. "What's the catch?"

"There is none."

"Wait! Just like that you can throw a switch that turns you from being in love with me to just accepting our friendship?"

"I refuse to allow my stupidity to ruin our final moments together."

Her eyes changed as she watched him. There seemed to be curiosity behind her blue peepers.

"What are you suggesting?"

"A field trip."

"What? To where?"

"There's this cool place just north of Baltimore that specializes in everything we'll need to turn this old house into a winter wonderland. So, I was just wondering—are you busy tonight?"

***

The rear seat of the pickup was full. Bags of garland, Christmas balls, twinkling lights, and a manger scene were waiting to be used.

"Are you sure you can afford all this stuff?"

"For years, I've been saving for a rainy day, and right now it's pouring." His smile raised her heartbeat a tad. "Or maybe I should say snowing. Do you see the flurries?"

"I do. They're beautiful."

"Oh Megan, just wait until we get back home. When the snow covers the hemlock trees in the yard, it's a sight to behold, like a Currier and Ives holiday scene."

"I've heard those names before. Were they artists?"

"The pair ran a well-renowned print shop and were famous for their lithographs. Lots of detail and color." The man grew quiet as he pointed his old Ford onto the interstate.

Megan was struggling to understand the change in Brendon's attitude after their argument.

"Why do you seem so chipper, after the bloody awful morning we had?"

"Because," he began without taking his eyes from the road, "I'm spending time with my best friend."

"Thanks, but why the change? You went from being unhappy that I'm returning to England to being euphoric tonight."

A smile grew on his lips.

"I'm confused. Is your joy because you secretly love to shop..." Megan hated to complete the sentence, but she needed to know, "or because you're relieved?"

"In what way?"

"That our engagement is really fake and you won't have to be shackled to me for the rest of your life?"

"Hold that thought." He steered the truck into the right lane and took the next exit. A coffee and donut shop sat near the off-ramp and he veered into the lot.

"What are we doing here?"

Brendon shifted into park and then turned so they were face to face. He switched on the interior lamps.

"What is going on?"

"I wanted to answer you. It might not come out the way I want it to, but I want you to see the honesty and sincerity on my face. First, please never think I wouldn't want to be with you." He took a deep breath before continuing. "I do love you and if it can't be the way I wish it would be, then it will be as your friend—as in a very close, lifelong friend."

"Brendon—"

"Please allow me to finish. I'm not sure if you realize how important you are to me. This friendship we share," he used his index finger to point first at his chest and then her heart, "will not end when you leave the USA. We will find a way to continue what we've begun. It might be hand-written letters or emails or video chats or maybe me visiting you in London, I don't know. But understand this, I refuse to allow you to walk out of my life."

She shook her head. "If this is a ploy to make me change my mind..."

"It's not, Megan. I thought about it long and hard this morning. I could be angry with you and end up kicking myself later for squandering the time we still have. I'm not so sure Jesus would act like that. We all strive to follow His footsteps—I mean, that's exactly what you're doing."

She eyed him with curiosity. "I must admit, after our argument, I never expected this."

"True friends find a way to work through their issues. You pointed out that we still have time to create memories we'll look back on forever. I don't want the biggest regret of my life to be that I threw away that opportunity. Of course, if this isn't what you want, tell me and, I'll stop immediately."

"Please don't," Megan replied quickly. "You're very important to me as well." *The most wonderful person I've ever known.*

"It will be hard and I'm sure I'll mess up, but I do love you, Megan. If it can't be romantically, then I'm determined to be the best friend you'll ever have."

Megan knew her cheeks were wet. The answer to her most private and secret prayers was right in front of her, yet so far away. *Lord, why does it have to be like this?*

"Did I answer your question about spending my life with you—as friends, of course?"

"Y-yes."

"We only have a few short weeks. Let's have the time of our lives. Agreed?" He stuck out his hand, but Megan ignored it. Instead, she threw her arms around him and squeezed harder than she ever had.

"Thank you for being my friend," she said in a squeaky voice. "I'm so lucky to have you."

"Maybe, but I'm the most blessed man God ever created, because I have your friendship."

Chapter Thirty

*T*aylor stood in the doorway, eyes almost popping from their sockets.

"Wow! I almost didn't recognize the place. What you and Brendon have done—it's amazing!"

"Thank you, but we had help." Megan lifted her hand to pay homage to Chloe, who was hanging decorative balls from the garland on the banister.

"Hey, Chloe. I thought your mother was home from the hospital." The girl nodded, but didn't answer.

Megan responded. "Jennifer was released, but she tires easily. We enjoy Chloe's company, so she's been hanging out here for a couple of hours in the evening, after getting her schoolwork done." The little girl came over and hugged Megan. "And Chloe is learning new things, such as how to make hot chocolate."

The child smiled and then asked Taylor, "Would you like a cup?"

"Yes, please."

The little girl ran into the kitchen.

"How's the decorating going at Chuck's house?"

"We're not nearly as far along as the two of you." There was a frown on Taylor's face. "I don't think we get along as well as you and my brother do. I guess it's a good thing we're not on the Hemlock Trail because we'd never be ready." Taylor studied Megan. "What's your secret?"

Megan felt her cheeks warm. "What do you mean?"

"What magical thing are you doing that makes you two get along so well?"

"We're best friends first."

Taylor's jaw dropped open. "First? Before what? Wait. Are you two..."

"Absolutely not! Your brother is a gentleman and need I remind you, Taylor, I am a lady." Megan exhaled before continuing. "We know we only have a short time left, so we don't argue. Our time together, that's what is important, not which one of us is right or if we get our own way."

"You two were meant for each other." Taylor shook her head. "I don't understand why or even how you'll be able to leave at the end of the marking period. After the closeness you two have, won't returning to London be a let-down?"

Megan picked up a decoration and spun away. She had to. "It will be good to be home." Megan hoped her voice sounded convincing.

Taylor suddenly stepped in front of her, the older woman's thumbs clearing the moisture dripping from Megan's eyes. "Liar."

"Don't say that."

"But it's true. One look at you and Brendon when you're together and anyone can see the two of you are in love."

"I'm not in love with your brother."

Taylor laughed. "I used to be your best friend, until Brendon came along. Would you do me a favor?"

"What's that?"

"Would you look me in the eyes and tell me you're not head over heels in love with him?"

"Stop it, Taylor."

"I've never asked much of you. I simply want you to tell me the truth. Can you?"

"You know I can't." Megan sobbed and moved away, but Taylor grabbed her arm and pulled her into a tight hug.

"Stay, Megan. You are always welcome here. Why don't you just see where it goes? I know Brendon loves you. Were you aware of that?"

"He's already told me that, numerous times."

"Really?" It would be hard not to hear the excitement in Taylor's voice. "Did you confess your feelings to him?"

"No, and I never will."

"Why?"

"Because I can't marry him."

"I don't understand."

"Please drop the subject. He's not the man I'm supposed to be with."

"What?" Taylor's voice rose in volume and Megan could detect not only surprise, but anger. "Is there someone else you love more, or is it possible my brother just isn't good enough? I bet you can't name one man who would be better suited to share his life with you than Brendon. Can you?"

"Quit harassing me, Taylor. There will never be another man like Brendon, but I've decided to devote my life to helping others."

Her friend grew quiet for a few seconds. "Are you planning on becoming a nun?"

"No, but I want to focus my effort on assisting others."

"That's great news, but why can't you and Brendon do it together? Think of the team you would be. I think happy people make better joy givers."

"King and country! You sound like your brother now. Brendon used the same argument—almost word for word."

"We," Taylor stopped to laugh, "both said the same thing because it's true. Explain to me why you can't be with Brendon when he loves you and you love him. Love is all it takes."

"Right," Megan mumbled almost under her breath. "It also takes money."

"Excuse me? What did you say?"

"Uh," Megan fumbled as her face seared, "Nothing."

"You said money, didn't you?"

"N-no."

"How does not being with my brother relate to money? Could it be he's not rich enough to suit your wants?"

The kitchen door swung open and Chloe walked out, holding a cup of brown liquid topped with whipped cream. Before turning to look at the girl, Taylor shot Megan the stink eye.

"Here's your hot chocolate, Miss Taylor."

"Thank you, Chloe."

"Oh, look at the time, young lady. Brendon will be in from the field in a few minutes." Megan glanced in Taylor's direction. "We were going to stop for pizza before taking Chloe home. Would you like to join us?" Megan hoped the answer would be no.

"Thanks for the offer, but I only stopped by to pick up a few things. I'll be spending the rest of the week at Chuck's place. Hopefully, we'll have the house decorated by Thanksgiving Day." Taylor's face softened. "Why don't you and Brendon drop by a little later? I'd love to finish this conversation."

Megan read between the lines. Getting together would be nice, but it was better to avoid the conversation Taylor wanted to have. Why? Because Megan's determination was beginning to crumble. *How* will *I be able to walk away from Brendon?*

Megan composed herself before replying, "We have a lot to do tonight. Brendon wants to get his old trains set up, you know, for the Hemlock Trail."

"I see," Taylor said as she nodded her head. "Anything for the greater good, huh?"

Chapter Thirty-one

"*J*ennifer seemed extremely tired today. That's got to be tough for Chloe," Brendon commented as he carried the box of model trains into the living room. His heart went out not only to Jennifer, but the little girl as well.

"It was nice of you to invite them to spend Thanksgiving with us. I've never experienced anything like our festivity today. We don't celebrate this holiday back home." Megan's lips pulled to one side of her face. "You Americans sure are a strange bunch."

"Right, and this coming from a girl who lives in a country with an honorary king and more dukes and duchesses than you can shake a stick at."

"Your country makes a holiday of shooting off fireworks in July."

"Duh, only as a way to celebrate our independence from your old King George. What about you Brits, making such a fuss about having tea every afternoon? Here in America, we drink our coffee while we work."

"At least we don't make predictions about how long winter will last by waiting to see if an oversize rodent sees his shadow."

"Americans don't roll blocks of cheese down a hill for fun."

Brendon could see Megan was trying to think of a good comeback. He intervened.

"It's a great thing you and I are so close. Together, we'll have to help each other muddle through the idiosyncrasies of the two greatest nations in the world."

His beautiful friend grew quiet as she looked through the box of model trains. "Do you really believe our friendship will survive the test of time?"

"I do."

"Even after I leave and Trina makes her play for you? She's in love with you, you know."

"But I'm in love with you, not her."

He detected moisture in her eyes. "Would we have made it, you know, if this engagement was real?"

"No. We wouldn't have just made it. I believe with all my heart we'd have one of the greatest love stories of all time. What do you think?"

She shook her head and held up a tiny model locomotive. "I see the legend reads Western Maryland. Is that a great rail company in the US?"

"The Western Maryland got absorbed by bigger companies in the early 1980s. America may not have all those centuries of history to look back on as Great Britain does, but we do get nostalgic over certain things. For people like me, we hold on to America's rail heritage." Brendon hesitated while he inspected one of the locomotives. "I guess the only thing that remains the same is change."

"I think you're right."

"That was a nice attempt to avoid answering my question."

Megan stared at him strangely. "What question?"

"If this was real, what would our relationship be?"

"I'd prefer not to answer."

"May I ask why?"

She was holding one of the miniature rail cars in her hand. "One day, you would have found out the real me isn't as special as you believe."

"Nonsense. I don't see how that would happen." He set down the toy train, and then moved to hold her hands. "Megan, to me you are the most wonderful woman God ever created."

"Right. I could never hold a candle to Trina. She has the perfect figure while I look more and more like the Queen every day. That is, just before Her Majesty passed away."

"Beauty is in the eye of the beholder. I want you to stop doing something."

"What's that?"

"Projecting Trina into my life. She was the biggest mistake I ever made. I wish I never would have met her." He grabbed a pencil from the counter and stuck it into his cast, rubbing it back and forth furiously.

"Stop that."

"It itches."

Megan studied his face. "You should be with someone."

"I am with someone—you!"

"But we're not ending up together."

His spirit tumbled as they stood there holding hands and facing each other. Something had a grip on Megan and he needed to understand what it was. If he could find out, Brendon might be able to develop a plan to overcome it.

"What do you want most in life?"

"To help others." Megan's response had been immediate.

"You're already doing that, at least in my eyes. Tell me what you would do if there was nothing to hold you back and you had every resource you wanted at your fingertips."

"I would make it easier for people who struggle every day to overcome the burdens they face just so they can live."

"Quite noble. Give me an example."

"Take Jennifer, for example. Her medications cost a lot, so much that she's forced to make a decision between buying them or providing food for Chloe."

"And you would what, pay for her prescriptions?"

"Yes."

"Is that all, or is there more?"

Megan stared at him with confused eyes. "What do you mean?"

"If you resolved her predicament, would that satisfy your desire to help others?"

"There will always be someone who is needy."

"Exactly. And *you* can't help them all."

Before Megan could respond, an alert sounded on her cell. He watched as she quickly glanced at its screen. Megan's eyes almost popped out of her head.

"If you'll excuse me, I need to take care of this."

"Everything okay?"

"Maybe. I'll let you know in a bit." With those words, she headed for the stairs.

Chapter Thirty-two

*M*egan ran to her room and locked the door. George the fourth's text had indicated he was ready to talk about her earlier message. Forcing herself to calm down, she awaited his invitation to join him on a video chat. After an almost five-minute delay, the invite came. Megan quickly accepted and the face of the man she would have to marry appeared on her screen.

"Megan, my love. Aren't you a looker tonight? I can't wait to see you wearing nothing, except maybe satin and lace."

She ignored his suggestive comment. "Good evening, George. Do you have an answer to my request?"

"Of course, I do. After all, I am a solicitor. You are getting quite a deal in the husband department."

"Can we stick to answering my request?"

The young man sighed. "Fine, but I want to have you tell me what I want to hear first."

"And that is?"

"Those three little words. I refuse to answer you until you say it."

Go drop dead? Instead, the control freak wanted her to utter words she would never mean.

"Fine. I love you." Even though she'd rushed the words, Megan fought back the urge to run to the sink and scrub her vocal cords with mechanic's hand soap.

"That wasn't so hard, was it? And I will feel the same way you do, in time."

I find it difficult to believe you are capable of love. "Now, about my request?"

"Yes, well, let me reiterate what you asked. You are requesting an advance on your inheritance—is that correct?"

"Yes. My request is time sensitive. I need ten thousand pounds."

"The earliest I can release those funds would be in about thirteen months."

Megan felt her face heat. "What? Why?"

"The will specifically dictated you may access six-point-six-seven percent of the total on the first anniversary after our wedding and the exact amount on each subsequent anniversary."

"This isn't right. I can't believe my grandmother would do this to me."

George frowned in a manner Megan suspected was supposed to show empathy. "That was her final wish."

Megan was becoming angrier and angrier by the second.

"You seem distraught. Do you need a loan, my dear?"

"What would the terms be?"

He quickly responded and Megan knew he'd thought this out. She blushed at his words.

"Certainly not! I will never do that."

"We'll be married soon."

"Don't expect me to fulfill that request—ever."

He laughed, which infuriated Megan. "If you change your mind, say the word. I could have the funds wired to your account the next day after receiving the video." An expression of curiosity slowly covered his face. "Might I ask why you need such a large sum?"

"A friend of mine can't afford the medication she needs."

"Ah, America can only dream of having such an exemplary healthcare system as we Brits enjoy. Let's brainstorm some options for you. You could petition the court system on behalf of your friend."

"I don't know enough about the legal system here."

"Right. You could ask your so-called American friends to offer aid."

"Taylor is a teacher and Brendon is a farmer. I don't believe they would have that much extra money sitting around."

"Charitable services?"

This was frustrating. George was not trying to help—he was simply belittling her. "I've gone down that path. While providing some assistance, it's simply not enough."

"Perhaps then, you should take out a loan. That seems to be the easiest solution."

"An even simpler way would be for the man I'll be marrying to help out. After all, you love me, don't you?" *Gag me with a spoon.* Even expressing those words made her queasy.

His face sobered and Megan wondered at that. "Let's not kid ourselves. I am simply marrying you at your grandmother's request. But, if you're lucky, I might fall in love with you—someday." He shot her a wink.

"Why are we even getting married?"

"It's the only way you can get your inheritance, so realize I am doing this as a favor—to you." He hesitated briefly and then a wide smile covered his face. "Of course, our union could be as mutually enjoyable for you as it will be for me."

"That means you're not going to help me?"

"My hands are tied," he replied with a shrug. "But per chance, you might reconsider my more than benevolent offer as a way to advance you the funds you need immediately."

"Fat chance on that. After all, one of us has to have morals and we both know it's not you." Megan disconnected before he could reply.

Chapter Thirty-three

*B*rendon waited in his truck for Megan. Chloe was already in the rear seat, working on homework. His brow furrowed. Chloe's mother Jennifer had less energy every day. He and Megan brought her home with them every evening now, returning the child to her mother just before bed.

He loved taking care of the little girl with Megan. Hopefully, this was a preview of what their family life would be like. *What's going to happen to Chloe if Megan really does leave?* Because Brendon knew his heart would be shattered on the ground, would he have the energy to continue assisting the child? He glanced in the rearview and the girl looked up, sending him a smile.

There had to be a way he could discover Megan's compulsion to return to Britain. He knew her well enough to understand the lady wasn't telling him the complete truth. *Yes, her desire is to help others, but there's something else going on here.* If he could determine exactly what it was...

"Can you check my homework, Mr. Brendon?"

Chloe's request interrupted his thoughts.

"Sure, sweetheart."

Chloe handed him the assignment. Brendon had just finished reviewing the sheet when Megan appeared. A shiver ran up his spine when he caught a glimpse of her face.

"Is something wrong?"

"No, I, uh, just a bad day, that's all. Can we leave?"

"Sure. Did something happen at school? If you want to talk, I'd love to listen."

"No, uh, it wasn't school. Look, I'm going to need a few minutes alone when we get to the farm."

"What's going on?"

"You wouldn't understand."

Brendon took a deep breath. "Try me. I'm your best friend."

"Please don't put any more pressure on me than I already have." He could hear the angst in her voice.

"That's not what I'm trying to do. I'm simply—"

She grasped his good arm. "I understand what you said, and it's true. You are the best friend I've ever had. But I need to calm myself and take a few moments to reflect."

"On what, Megan?" *Your life, your future?*

"It's extremely personal."

Brendon didn't push and remained quiet through the rest of the ride. There was a lot on the agenda tonight. Sunday was the day of the Hemlock Trail and it was already Friday. He and Megan had planned on starting to create the mountains of desserts for the event this evening. Taylor and Chuck would be coming over on Saturday to assist in making pies and cakes, but tonight it was just Megan, Brendon and Chloe. To everyone's surprise, the signup list among the area churches indicated over five hundred people now planned to attend. This evening, the strategy was to bake cookies, scones and tarts. Yet there was something even more pressing and that was getting to the bottom of whatever had spooked Megan so badly.

Brendon muttered to himself. "What is it, Lord? Show me how to help her."

Over the last week or two, he'd picked up on the increased frequency with which Megan's cell drew her attention. In the past, she would often ignore when her phone pinged with messages. But now? It seemed that each time the device sounded, everything else had to stop. And one thing he'd deduced—she seemed more frightened each time she looked at her phone.

"Who is constantly texting her?" Brendon didn't know, but planned to find out—when the time was right.

***

After returning to the farm, Megan bundled up before taking the Gator. Her idea was to head off for the far edge of the Davis's farm and meditate. Thankfully she wasn't alone. Orville had faithfully followed, jumping on the four-wheeler and resting his head on her shoulder as she drove.

Megan reached the destination and quickly looked back on the house—or rather where it should be seen. Luckily, the edge of this field was in a small valley, so the farmhouse was hidden from view.

She hopped off the Gator and leaned against a massive rock at the side of the corn field. A strong wind chilled her spirit even further.

"God, I need Your help. I want to do Your will, however, I'm struggling. By getting the inheritance, I realize I could help so many people, but I'm not sure if I can pay the price." Since their video chat, George had constantly been sending her messages, sometimes with pictures or videos attached, concerning his plans for her. When she ignored George and failed to respond, her silence apparently aggravated him. While those types of messages were disgusting, of a more frightening nature were his threats to come to America and find out 'what was going on'. *Oh, how that man disturbs me!*

"I don't believe I can go through with marrying George. To do the things he's suggested after marriage is pure evil."

Her thoughts suddenly drifted to Brendon and how the man treated her. Instead of making demands or trying to be in control, Brendon simply shared the joy of life with Megan. It was plain to see that he truly loved her. *I love you, too, Brendon.*

"You know there is nothing I would like more in life than to spend it with Brendon here, in America. Would it hurt Your plans if I would forego the inheritance and stay with Brendon? We could make a difference just where we are."

Clearing her mind, she waited for God's response. Tiny bits of something began to touch her cheeks. Looking up, she realized it was beginning to snow. She listened intently for the Lord's voice, but the only sound was the soft whisper of the flakes falling on dead leaves.

"Help me, God. You know my heart's desire is to be with Brendon." Silence followed, but a feeling grew in her heart. A union with Brendon would be bliss, but there was more at stake here than Megan's happiness. Five million pounds would go a long way to help other needy souls.

"Am I simply a modern-day Paul? I mean, the man was persecuted, beaten and jailed for spreading the Gospel. He didn't ask for the job, but You gave it to him." Megan paused to reflect. "I didn't ask for these funds, yet You provided them. If I turn my back on the inheritance and make a future with Brendon, would You be disappointed in me?"

The words of Matthew 19:21 suddenly filled her mind, *'If you want to be perfect, go, sell your possessions and give to the poor, and you will have treasure in Heaven.'* The young man in the passage couldn't because he had great wealth, prompting Jesus to tell His disciples, *'It is easier for a camel to pass through the eye of a needle, than for the wealthy to enter into the kingdom of Heaven.'*

"It would be different if You hadn't allowed Grandmother to leave me this inheritance. But now that it's mine, I feel You are telling me that I need to go through with it." *Even if it means I'll have to marry George?* Sadly, even so. But there was more at stake than her worries—Brendon's heart was her main concern.

She wiped her eyes. Megan's only hope was for Brendon to find happiness elsewhere. After Megan arrived in Britain, she would force Brendon from her mind and immediately sever all ties with the American. Her plan for this evening was her first step in helping him forget. After all, it was what would be best for him. *Right?*

Chapter Thirty-four

"*L*et's cover the peanut butter batter so we can set it outside."

"Why, Mr. Brendon?" Chloe was so cute with those big eyes.

"My sister taught me that these types of cookies come out better if the mixture is chilled first." Pushing the door open, the chill of the December night rushed at him. A quick glance at the yard revealed snow falling quietly. He set the bowl on top of the shoe rack, just high enough so that Orville couldn't disturb it.

"Where are you, Megan?" he whispered into the night.

She'd headed outside almost two hours ago. The girl had to be freezing. *What's going through your mind? Please let her share her worries and struggles with me, Lord.* Brendon began to wonder if his gamble of trying to win her heart by being the best friend she could imagine might fail. *Megan can't leave—she mustn't.*

The far-off echo of the Gator's engine drifted on the wind. Focusing his eyes on the fields, he caught the glimmer of the headlights in the distance.

"Finally!" Quickly stepping inside, he called for Chloe. "Hey kiddo, Miss Megan is on her way back. How about I dip the stew while you make the hot chocolate?"

"Okay." The little girl was a big help. Brendon was glad he'd put beef stew in the slow cooker that morning. The oven was already on, so he slipped in a tray of biscuits. Between them, the meal was fully prepared when Megan stepped through the door. His heart tumbled as he caught sight of her expression. It was easy to see she'd been crying.

"Everything okay?"

Instead of replying, she simply nodded her head.

"You sure?"

"Just peachy."

Before he could inquire farther, Chloe said, "Mr. Brendon and me mixed up the batter for the cookies. We made chocolate chip and sugar cookie and peanut butter. I can't wait to taste them. After supper, can we have some for dessert after we bake them? Mr. Brendon said we're making one hundred-twenty dozen."

The child excitedly spoke of the cookies they'd bake. As Brendon gazed at the young woman, his heart dropped. He could see it in her eyes... she'd made her decision. Megan *was really* planning to leave.

It was a good thing their young friend was with them, because her exuberance broke the silence. Brendon was relieved when the girl asked if they could listen to Christmas carols on the radio.

After he'd loaded all the dinner dishes in the dishwasher, the cookie making process began in earnest. Chloe and Megan were in charge of placing the cookies on the baking sheet. It was Brendon's job to shuttle the treats in and out of the oven and then cool the cookies on the table.

"Where did we decide to store the cooled cookies?" he asked Megan.

"We talked about stacking them in those boxes," she replied while pointing to a large number of white containers waiting in the living room.

"Do you want me to, or are you planning on doing it?"

He thought it odd that she glanced at her watch. "Actually..." A sudden knock on the door caught his attention.

"Right on time," he thought he heard Megan whisper. When he looked up, she nodded in the direction of the noise and then turned away. "Could you answer that?"

"Okay." He walked over and swung it open. Brendon knew his jaw must have hit the ground when he saw who was standing there—Trina Lewis.

***

Megan took in the scene. Brendon's body language easily indicated his anger.

"What do you want?" he growled at the guest.

"May I come in?"

The snow must have increased because numerous flakes decorated her well-styled hair. A shudder ran down Megan's spine. Trina looked exquisite tonight in jeans and an apricot-colored top. There was no doubt about it—Brendon's old flame was a beautiful woman. Megan's hope was that Brendon would take note of how stunning Trina looked.

Brendon didn't answer, so Megan stepped over. "Come in, Trina. Let me hang up your wrap."

The man whipped around to face Megan.

"I asked Trina to give us a hand this evening," she responded before he could inquire.

"Why?"

"Because we have a lot of cookies to bake and Trina volunteered."

After hugging her 'friend', Megan led Trina to the kitchen. Several batches of baked cookies covered the table.

"We each have a role in this process. I'm hoping you could box and label the treats."

"Excuse me," Brendon asked out loud. "May I have a word with you, Megan?"

"You have cookies ready to come out in less than one minute."

"I can handle that if you two need a moment." Trina's smile displayed pure eagerness to assist.

"Thanks," Brendon grumbled before grabbing Megan's arm and pulling her with him to the living room. His grip was firm.

Out of earshot of the work room, Megan yanked her arm free. "You're hurting me."

"I apologize for that, but tell me why she's here."

"Trina offered to be of assistance."

"She's a snake, Megan. You and I have enough going on between us without her complicating matters. The only thing that witch wants is to drive a wedge between us."

"Open your eyes, Brendon. She cares for you. Put yourself in her shoes. Trina loves you, and I believe she always will. She's resigned herself not only to stand on the sidelines and watch you and I be together, but she's happy for us."

"I'm so confused by what's happening here with you, with us, but if this is your plan, forget it."

"Why?"

"That woman broke my heart, time and again. She destroyed the relationship I had with Noelle."

Before Megan could respond, the kitchen door swung open. Chloe walked into the room.

"We're done with the chocolate chip cookies. Miss Trina wants to know which ones are next."

"I'll be right there, sweetie."

Chloe departed and Megan turned to face Brendon.

He spoke before she could. "You're really going to leave me, aren't you?"

"I have no choice."

"You always do." He gently took her hand and led her a few steps to her right. "Look up," he whispered.

Megan's throat tightened when she realized they were directly under the mistletoe.

"Kiss me, Megan." The sensation of his trembling fingers against the back of her neck as he softly pulled her toward him was one she knew she would always remember.

"No, we can't do this."

From mere millimeters away, Brendon answered. "It's a time-honored tradition. Am I not worthy of a simple kiss?"

"Brendon," she pleaded, "this isn't fair. Can we—"

The soft touch of his lips stopped all resistance. Unwillingly, her arms wrapped around his head and they melted together. Time stopped as bliss rained down on them.

He slowly pulled away, but Megan wouldn't allow him to release her. She invited Brendon to her lips time and again. It was as if he were part of her, a blessed union she wished would never end.

"Oh, this is what 'needing a moment' really means, huh?" Trina's laughter-laced words forced them apart.

Brendon released Megan and rushed past the pretty woman into the kitchen.

Trina's expression faded. "I'm sorry. I didn't mean to interrupt you two."

"It's fine," Megan lied. "Be there in a jiffy."

Trina nodded and departed.

Despite his absence, the sensation of Brendon's lips still tingled on hers. More confused than ever, she collapsed onto a chair. The resilience to follow her plan was crumbling by the second.

"What do I do now, Lord?" She waited for a reply and could picture God up in Heaven on His throne—laughing at her. "Is this Your blessing or the devil tempting me?"

The words of Hebrews 13:5 quickly filled her mind. *"Keep your lives free from the love of money and be content with what you have, because God has said, 'Never will I leave you; never will I forsake you.'"*

"What? I don't want the money for me. You know how George makes me sick. There's no way I'd go through with this sham if it weren't for the money. There are so many who need assistance. I can ease the pain of quite a few with that inheritance. What about them?"

New words appeared in her mind, this time from Ezekiel 34:26. *I will make them and the places surrounding my hill a blessing. I will send down showers in season; there will be showers of blessing.*

As if on a television screen, yet another verse entered the conversation – II Corinthians 9:7. These words struck a chord in her heart. *'Each of you should give what you have decided in your heart to give, not reluctantly or under compulsion, for God loves a cheerful giver.'*

Even with the millions her inheritance offered, she would never be happy married to George.

Her mouth fell open. One last thought entered her mind, along with the image of Brendon's face.

'For I know the plans I have for you, plans to prosper you and not to harm you, plans to give you hope and a future.'

"Could it be as simple as that?" That verse had been the theme for the previous week's sermon. This time no more words filled her thoughts, but a warmth surrounded her, as if the Creator was holding her close. In that moment, Megan knew everything would be all right.

Chapter Thirty-five

*O*n Saturday morning, Megan woke happier than she ever remembered. After a long night of peaceful rest, the path forward was finally clear in her mind. Closing her eyes, Brendon's smiling face reappeared before her. How she'd wanted to talk to him last night, but because of Trina's interruption, they hadn't had the chance.

After composing herself, she'd returned to the kitchen. Brendon was helping Chloe collect her things. She'd been disappointed with his words, but that didn't matter. The man was obviously stressed by the impending Hemlock Trail.

"Is it time to take our friend home already?"

"Yes," he'd replied. *"Since we'll be using the equipment shed as a gathering and serving location, I'm going to clear the farm implements from the building when I get back."*

"You decided to do that tonight instead of tomorrow?"

"Moving the implements is just the first part. The space needs to be cleaned and then decorated. In the morning, I'll pick up the tables, chairs and other stuff from the rental company. To me, it makes sense to get a jump on it."

"I see. Would you like a hand?"

"No, thanks. I'll be using the tractor to relocate everything."

After the kiss they'd shared, she wanted to be close with him. *"I could help. After all, I do drive a pretty mean tractor. We both know the reason was because I had a great teacher."*

The look he'd shot back told her he was upset, but why? Was it because Trina interrupted them or because Megan had invited the woman in the first place?

"I appreciate that, but it will go a lot faster if I do it myself. Besides, the wind is kicking up and the snow's starting to lay." He nodded in his ex's direction. *"I think the two of you will need a couple more hours to finish up. So, good night. Talk to you in the morning."*

Megan knew she should have felt disappointed, but a warmth grew in her chest. After all this time, the winds of her heart were changing. God was answering her prayers, and today was the first day of the rest of her life. As a tribute to the Almighty, she would brighten the lives of those around her, giving of herself instead of money.

Interrupting her thoughts, the sound of a small engine roared outside. Quickly glancing through the window, she located Brendon. He was using a leaf blower to clean out the shed.

Happiness cascaded through her body. Today would be busy, but Megan couldn't wait. When they had a moment alone, she would tell Brendon she planned to stay, but that wasn't the most important thing. She would share her true feelings. Everything they'd been pretending to be was true. Megan would tell Brendon she wanted to marry him.

But first, she had another task to complete. Grasping her cell, she opened her texting application. Selecting the thread with George the fourth, she quickly typed the following:

> George, it's over. I've come back to my senses. Keep Grandmother's money for yourself. I've discovered something more valuable than silver or gold. I will not be coming back to London, so please close the lease on her old flat. You and I never would have worked anyway. Goodbye.

Megan couldn't help but giggle to herself. She blocked George's number and smiled in the mirror.

"My life has finally begun, Lord. Thank You for opening my eyes." Hugging herself, she fell back on the bed. Megan's mind was clear and her heart light. She couldn't wait to tell Brendon.

***

There was so much to do. The equipment shed was filthy. He really should use the pressure sprayer to clean the floor, but there wasn't enough time. Besides, the water might freeze and create a slip hazard.

One thing about all the work, it took some of the edge off the pain in his heart. *She's really going to leave?* When Megan said she had no choice, he'd panicked. Brendon's heart had taken a gamble and he kissed Megan under the mistletoe. His hope was the kiss might have rekindled the magic of their first one in church. That embrace last night would forever be one of his favorite memories—so sweet and right. But had it been enough to change her mind?

It hadn't been time to take Chloe home, but Brendon knew he'd been about to lose control. Five more minutes and he would have been on his knees, begging Megan to stay. And of course, Trina would have been there to witness it all. He shook his head and glanced at the horizon.

"Father, if there's any way possible, please change Megan's mind. I love that woman." His mind drifted back to the previous week's sermon and Jeremiah 29:11. Did God really have plans for Brendon's life? And if He did, was a life with Megan in God's plan?

The ringing of his cell stopped the pity party. Pulling it from his pants pocket, he noted the caller's ID. *Jennifer?* Why would Chloe's mother be calling him this morning? Brendon depressed the accept button.

"Hello?"

"Brendon, thank God you answered." She sounded horrible.

"Don't you normally call Megan?"

"Yes, but she's not answering and this is urgent."

"Are you okay?"

"No. I'm really sick. I spoke with my doctor and he wants to admit me to the hospital again." Jennifer's voice started to break. "I don't know what to do about Chloe."

That changed everything. Preparations would need to wait.

"I'll see if I can find Megan. If not, I'll be there in twenty minutes. Don't worry about anything, we'll take care of your daughter."

"Thank you. Friends like you are a gift."

He disconnected and ran to the house. His urgency must have startled Orville, because the dog began barking at him. Not even stopping to remove the dirty boots on his feet, he threw open the door. A startled Megan ran from the kitchen. A smile quickly lit up her face when she saw him.

"Where's your phone?"

"I, uh, don't know. Maybe it's still upstairs. Why?"

Brendon briefed Megan on the call. Before he was even done, she was reaching for her coat.

"That poor child. My heart goes out to her."

"Mine, too. I told Jennifer not to worry, we'll take care of Chloe."

"Taylor and Chuck are coming over to help bake. Maybe we can make a party of it."

"Let's call Chuck's phone."

"Why?"

"Time's ticking. I'm going to need help setting up."

She didn't answer immediately, so Brendon chanced a quick look. She seemed perplexed.

"I thought we were going to decorate the building together. Now you don't want my help?"

"I didn't say that. It will take a while to get it prepped. I'm hoping by the time you're finished baking, we'll be ready to decorate."

"That's good. I was afraid you didn't want me anymore. Uh... I mean my help."

He rolled his eyes. "You know that will never be true. Even if you leave, I'll still need you—and I'll always want you." He hoped his words might make her reflect.

Megan hesitated before responding.

"It's going to be a long, hectic day, but before it's through, you and I need to talk."

"About what?"

The sudden warmth of her fingers against his hand startled him. Brendon's head swiveled to see her face. He couldn't recall a more radiant smile. Even more surprising was her quick kiss.

"About our future... together... as in this being real... and forever."

Chapter Thirty-six

Megan stood by the window, waiting for Brendon to return after finishing his morning chores. As she sipped her coffee, her mind returned to the joy of the previous evening. It had been close to eleven when Taylor and her fiancé departed. After baking, the five of them—Taylor, Chuck, Chloe, Brendon and Megan, had turned the equipment shed into a place of wonder.

Today's forecast was calling for light snow, which, coupled with the inch or two already on the ground, set the stage for the holiday celebration.

Noise from upstairs told her Chloe was awake. The poor child needed stability in her life. Megan was fully aware that Jennifer's condition might never improve. Since Megan would now be staying here, she and Brendon could help the little girl. They would provide her a safe place to stay, and give her comfort in dealing with the deteriorating condition of her mother.

Moving to the coffee maker, she inserted a hot chocolate pod. By the time Chloe stepped through the kitchen door, Megan had the cocoa ready.

"Good morning, precious."

"Morning, Miss Megan. Something smells good. I'm hungry."

"I prepared a quiche. As soon as Mr. Brendon returns, the three of us will eat breakfast."

"May I have a cookie to hold me over?"

"Of course." She retrieved two chocolate chip treats from the container on the counter. "I think I'll join you." She plopped down next to the child and the pair enjoyed the delicacy.

The rumble of the Gator sliced through the silence of the morning. Megan popped a coffee pod in the machine and by the time Brendon walked in, she had breakfast on the table.

"Merry Christmas, everyone," Brendon greeted as he walked in. After hanging his coat, he dropped a quick kiss on Megan's lips.

"Today's not Christmas, is it?"

"No. Chloe," Brendon replied with a smile. "Next Saturday is the official date, but it's okay to feel the spirit beforehand." The gentleman shot Megan an award-winning smile before continuing. "You know, since you'll be staying with Megan and I for the holiday, we should get you a stocking to hang by the fireplace. Would you like that?"

"I'd love that," exclaimed Chloe as she clapped joyfully.

"Good." Brendon offered them his hands. Chloe grasped both his and Megan's. When Megan took Brendon's, he gave it a light squeeze.

"Heavenly Father. Good morning. We offer our thanks for the food we are about to receive and for the beautiful hands that prepared it. As I walked in the house earlier, I noticed the snow flurries You sent. It seems even nature is celebrating the birth of Jesus. Today will be quite busy for us with the Hemlock Trail. Please let our hearts be open to Your spirit as we welcome our guests. Fill them with not only the desserts that have been prepared, but with the wonder of the season and the joy of the birth of Your son. Amen."

"Amen." Megan's heart was full of anticipation for not only the day, but their future. "When do you want to start getting ready?"

"After my shower, I'll head out to the shed and fire up the propane heaters. Then maybe the three of us can carry out the food. Perhaps you and Chloe could work on displaying the goodies. While you're doing that, I'll run into town and pick up the flowers and ice."

"Sounds good. Chuck and Taylor are set to arrive about eleven. We agreed they'll man the house while we host the party in the equipment building, right?"

"That was our plan."

"What am I supposed to do?" asked Chloe.

"What would you like to do, princess?" Brendon reached over to touch her nose with his finger.

"Hang around with Miss Megan."

"That works for me. Wait, are you going to be her mini-Meg?"

The girl giggled as she nodded. Brendon shot Megan a wink.

She stared at the man with wonder. His vision, his organization and his aura were amazing. *Thank You, God, for changing my heart.* "I can't believe we're pulling this off."

His look was humorous, with one eyebrow raised high. "I can't believe you would ever doubt us. After all, God brought us together for a reason. And never forget, Megan, together, you and I can do anything."

Chapter Thirty-seven

*T*he Hemlock Trail was in full swing. Dozens of cars were parked along the lane. Perhaps fifty people stood chatting inside the equipment shed as they enjoyed the lovingly prepared cookies, pies and cakes.

Brendon rubbed his sore arm. The snow made his bones ache. Still, he couldn't help but watch in wonder as Megan flitted around like a social butterfly. And of course, Chloe seemed to be attached to his fiancée at the hip. *Thank You, God, for Megan and for keeping her here.* His life had never been so happy or his heart so full.

"You guys did a wonderful job preparing for today."

Brendon didn't have to look to see who spoke the words—it was Trina.

"Thank you for all your assistance," he replied while keeping his eyes on Megan.

"I didn't do much, really. Now Megan, on the other hand, she's a dynamo." She paused briefly. "I need to say this, so please don't stop me." Trina moved so they were eye to eye.

"Please don't do this."

"Wait. I'm not trying to ruin the joy of the day. When Megan brought you back to church, I was surprised. I thought her intentions weren't real."

"They were and are. Look, Trina—"

"Please don't interrupt me."

Brendon sighed heavily. "Go ahead."

"The night she leaked it to me that the two of you were engaged, it didn't feel right. And the way you kissed so passionately in church felt fake."

"It wasn't."

The pretty woman smiled at him. "I understand that now. Anyone who spends more than a minute with you can see you're both in love and belong together. Yet there's more to your girl than meets the eye."

"Yeah? What's that?"

"Her heart. I believed when she started inviting me to hang out with her, it was to rub my nose in the fact you belong to her. I'm certain you've shared with her how I've treated you, yet she wanted us to be friends. Do you know why?"

"No."

"Megan has a pure and love-filled spirit." Trina nodded in the direction of his fiancée. "See how great of a hostess she is, making everyone feel welcome? And how she treats Jennifer's daughter as if she were her own?" Trina sighed.

"What's your point?"

"You've found an angel—someone much better than I'll ever be. I'll always love you, but I'll be the first to admit—Megan is the girl you belong with. Even I can see that. I hope you realize how incredibly blessed you are and that you should always hold on to her."

As Trina stared at him, he noted a solitary tear rolling down her cheek. She blotted it with a tissue. "Well, thanks for listening. I've got to get moving. Looks like we're getting low on punch."

He watched Trina retreat. For the first time in years, he was glad she was here. Maybe it was time to unharden his heart and forgive the woman.

"Hello, love. I saw you and Trina chatting. Are you okay?" Megan stood beside him, offering a cup of hot chocolate.

"She was just telling me how lucky I am to have found you."

The width of Megan's smile filled his heart. "I'm the fortunate one. I can't wait..."

Megan's words trailed off and the smile departed. Her face began to redden. Her eyes were focused over his left shoulder to the doorway.

"No, please no," she whispered through trembling lips.

Brendon whipped around to find a tall man making a beeline right for Megan. From his polished shoes to the top hat he sported, he seemed out of place. His wardrobe reminded Brendon of something Fred Astaire might have worn in a musical.

Protectively, Brendon stepped between the man and Megan. "May I help you?"

"No, thank you. I wish to speak with Megan." His voice was loud and carried throughout the building. He paused and Brendon noted most people had grown silent.

He sensed all eyes were on them. "Would you care for some dessert first?"

"No. You see, I've come here to collect my betrothed."

"Wh-what? Excuse me, but what did you just say?"

The crowd was so quiet, one could hear a pin drop.

"I'm here to take Megan with me. Were you aware this woman has agreed to be my wife?" The man paused and cast a diminutive expression at Brendon. "I've come to stop this American folly, retrieve her and take her back to London where she belongs. There's not much time to go before our wedding and then," the man said with a lusty smile, "the honeymoon begins."

In disbelief, Brendon pivoted to face Megan. "Do you know this man?"

"Unfortunately, yes."

"Is it true you agreed to be his wife?"

"Kind of, in a way. Let me explain..."

"When were you going to tell me this?" He couldn't help it. The volume of his voice seemed to raise itself.

A look of panic covered Megan's face. "Please, let me explain what happened."

Brendon's heart was breaking. He looked her right in the eyes. *All this time and she never breathed a word about this? What a fool I am!* "There was a time for explanations and truth—and that was before he showed up." Things were getting blurry. "I really misjudged you, didn't I?"

"Wait, we need to talk."

"No, Ms. McKenzie. The time for discussion is over." Brendon was about to lose control. He needed to get out of there—fast. "I wish I could say it was nice to have met you, but I won't lie. Have a great life."

He turned and headed for the door, but Megan grabbed his arm. "Brendon, please wait. I love you."

Ripping his limb from her grip, he could barely speak to her. "Get out of my way. All this time and you're no better than Trina. I just moved from one cheating woman to another."

"That's not true. Please listen to me." Tears were running down her cheeks as she touched his face.

Brendon pulled back and away from her. "I never want to see you again." He rushed away from her and this time she didn't follow. The building was completely silent except for Megan's sobs.

His heart begged him to stop and comfort her, but the hurt and anger of her betrayal forced him forward. Brendon ran from the warmth and comfort of the celebration into the cold outside. Flakes floated in the air, like the ashes of what was once his love for Megan.

Jumping into his truck, Brendon cast one last glance at the building. Megan stood at the doorway, obviously upset as she watched him. He shook his head and muttered, "Goodbye and good riddance." Brendon drove off into the snowy afternoon without looking back.

Chapter Thirty-eight

*I*t was difficult to catch her breath as Megan watched Brendon's old truck disappear down the drive. *God, you promised You had plans for my life. This can't be real. Please waken me from this nightmare.*

"Is *he* the reason you were planning on staying?" George's words were like salt rubbed into a wound.

"How dare you," Megan screamed as she whipped around. "What kind of a man are you?"

"The kind you're going to marry."

She slapped his face and a collective gasp rose from all those watching. "When donkeys fly. Why did you come here?"

The man softly rubbed his cheek. "To get what's rightfully mine. And that is you."

"You act like I'm some piece of property you can possess."

"If you want your inheritance, the will states you *must* marry me."

A movement off to her right captured her attention for a second. Taylor was standing there red-faced, holding Chloe. The child was upset. *I'll have to comfort her as soon as I rid myself of this rat.* A second glance revealed everyone in the building was engrossed in the issue. She turned her attention back to George.

"I don't believe Grandmother realized the curse she placed on my life by that requirement."

"What? Being married to me?" The man laughed and each chuckle raised her anger. "You are going to live a life of luxury."

"And perversion. I've seen what real love is... and what you are suggesting isn't."

George's laughter was now like nails on a chalkboard. "Love? Are you talking about that man who ran away at the first sign of adversity? Good riddance to him. He'll never be a tenth of the man I am. Consider yourself lucky, girl."

Megan raised her arm to smack him again, but George grabbed it.

"My, but you do have a temper. I'm looking forward to taming you and your spirit."

"Leave, now!"

"We can go together."

"No! This is where I'm staying."

"Ha! You've no reason to remain now. Your prince ran off like a dog with his tail between his legs."

"Don't you doubt this. I will find a way to heal things with Brendon. As for you, leave now."

"Or what, Megan? Let's be honest. You are coming with me." He grabbed both her arms and pulled her close.

A menacing growl filled the air. Quickly turning her head, Megan found Orville there. His hackles were standing on end and his teeth were bared. When the dog moved closer, George released her.

"Leave."

"Let me get this straight. You are not marrying me and you are not returning to London. Am I correct?"

"Yes, on both accounts."

"Since these were the two requirements, that means you must forfeit your inheritance."

"I don't care. I have everything I could ever want right here."

"And you're sure?"

She was so angry, Megan felt like throttling him. "As certain as God is in Heaven."

His 'I got my way' smile made her ill. There was no way Grandmother could possibly have known what a sick man George was. He reached into his coat pocket and extracted an envelope.

"Do you really want me out of your life?"

"Absolutely."

He offered her a pen and some papers he'd pulled from the pocket of his coat. "Sign this document and I'll be gone."

"What is this?"

"It's an affidavit."

"A what?"

"A written expression that you're abandoning all claims to your grandmother's inheritance."

"And that means you'll get everything?"

"Precisely. All five and a half million pounds. Your signature makes this a binding agreement. Unless you would rather be my wife."

It was all clear now. *He played me.* He was never serious about getting married. All those vile comments and suggestions he'd made were intended to make her say no. Since her grandmother's death, George's actions had been about stealing what should have rightfully been hers.

But that money isn't the true treasure. Without hesitation, Megan grabbed the paper, read it (because she would never trust this weasel), and then signed it.

She slammed the document against his chest. "There. Now be gone, or I'll tell this dog to tear you apart."

The man was smiling ear to ear. "As you wish." He turned to go, but instead looked back. "Such a shame. You would have been an exciting conquest."

As if the dog understood what the fiend had said, Orville growled louder and nipped at the man's pants. George literally ran from the building with the canine in hot pursuit.

I need to find Brendon. I have to make this right.

Taylor was suddenly before her and the expression on her friend's face wasn't pleasant. Megan noted Taylor had handed Chloe off to Trina. Taylor's words were angry as she hissed them.

"Let's go into the barn. You and I need to talk— now."

Chapter Thirty-nine

*B*rendon had headed south. He needed time to think, so he chose Harper's Ferry. It would be deserted and that was fine with him.

His was the only vehicle in the lot when he arrived. It dawned on him that this was the same location they'd visited after Megan told Trina they were engaged.

"How could I have been so blind? All this time and I don't even know her." *How could she be engaged to someone else, but act and kiss me the way she did?*

"This is like my experience with Trina all over again." He kicked at a pile of snow-covered leaves. "I should face it. I'm destined to be alone."

His cell rang—it was Megan. Silencing the device, he brushed the snow from a table and sat down.

It pained him to know he'd never hear her voice, hold her hand or laugh with her—ever again. Those blue eyes that twinkled when she smiled were gone for good. He'd never look deeply into them again as he held her.

Another call came on his device. This was from Taylor. Undoubtedly, his sister had heard about Megan's betrayal and wanted to comfort him. *There will be time for that later, sis.* Right now, he just needed to be alone. Brendon powered down the device and just listened to the world around him.

The hushed rumble of the river below was accented by the occasional rhythm of a hungry woodpecker. In the distance, the wail of the horn from a passing train somehow made the evening seem colder.

As he'd done many times before Megan reintroduced him to church, Brendon allowed his mind to focus on God and the wonder of nature. He pondered life and asked God why He'd planned for Brendon to always be alone. Megan's face kept appearing in his mind, and each time it did, he forced it out.

He sadly realized the world would go on, whether Megan was by his side or not. Turning his thoughts into himself, he prayed for serenity until he felt God's peace descend on him. It was as if the Almighty was saying 'this too shall pass'. Brendon knew God would be with him. At some point he closed his eyes and fell asleep, but his dreams went to a beautiful young Brit with a charming accent. And she walked beside him, their hands clasped together.

A hand grabbed his shoulder and shook him.

"Sir, are you okay?"

Brendon's eyes flew open. It was dark and he sensed that snow covered his jeans. A flashlight illuminated the area. The man in front of him wore the uniform of a park ranger, yet he looked slightly familiar. Brendon gave up trying to remember how he knew him.

"Are you with me, sir?"

"Yes, yes. I'm sorry. I must have fallen asleep. What time is it?"

"Almost eleven. This area was closed to visitors at dusk. I'm afraid you'll need to leave."

"I apologize. I guess the drama of the day got to me."

"What drama?"

For the next few minutes, Brendon poured out his heart to this stranger. The man cleared the snow from the picnic table and sat next to him, listening intently. It seemed odd that this stranger displayed such compassion.

"I guess I'm a basket case, huh?"

"Life can throw curveballs at us," the stranger answered. "I would suggest you hold tight to your faith and look for the good that will come out of this." The man stood and looked directly at Brendon. "And if I can offer one last piece of advice, it would be this. Be quick to forgive Megan. You never know the path others walk and the hidden struggles they endure."

Brendon nodded at the man's advice.

The ranger closed with, "Go in peace."

They shook hands and Brendon headed to his truck. In the lot, he found it strange that there were no other vehicles. Shouldn't there be one for the ranger? *Maybe he already left.* Brendon became even more puzzled when he realized there were no tire tracks.

"Isn't that peculiar? Maybe the man walked in and needs a lift."

Brendon retraced his steps to the picnic table. In disbelief, he noted only one set of footprints—his own.

"What? Who was that man?"

Glancing at the picnic table where they had sat together revealed the snow was intact.

"But I watched him brush it away."

And that was when it dawned on Brendon. The man had suggested he should be quick to forgive *Megan*—but how could that be? Brendon had never mentioned her name.

Chapter Forty

*I*t was just after midnight. Megan sat on the porch steps, accompanied by Orville. A bitter wind cut straight through her coat, gloves and hat.

"God, please bring Brendon back to me. I'll understand if he rejects me, but I've got to at least explain it to him. Hopefully, he'll react better than Taylor."

The woman who for years had been her best friend unloaded on Megan once they'd reached the barn. According to Brendon's sister, Megan was a liar, a cheat, an opportunist and unworthy of either her brother or staying at their farm.

Megan rubbed her gloves together to try and keep warm. Taylor had immediately canceled their participation in the Hemlock Trail, chased everyone out, then collected Chloe and the little girl's belongings. The last thing her friend did was warn Megan to be gone by the time the sun rose again. But the thing Taylor said that drove a knife in Megan's heart was when Taylor told her she hated Megan, never wanted to see her again and wished they'd never met.

By the time everyone departed, Megan had her belongings packed and was ready to leave. She had called for an Uber to take her to a motel. The house was silent. Sitting alone at the kitchen table, Megan felt someone's eyes on her. Glancing up, Trina emerged from the shadows. Their ensuing conversation had seemed unreal.

"What are you going to do?"

"Do I really have a choice?"

"Actually, you do."

"Right. Run home to England or jump off the first tall cliff I come to are the only options I see."

"Megan, let me give you some advice. Love— even a great love like you two share—takes work. There will be problems, and many times you'll both wonder if it's all worth it." Trina stopped and wiped her nose with a tissue. *"Here's my piece of wisdom. Love means everything in this world. Leave without talking to Brendon and you'll regret that decision for the rest of your life."*

"He hates me. Brendon believes everything I said or did was a lie."

"Maybe it was, and that's not for me to know— but you should tell him the truth. You owe it to Brendon to explain what happened."

"I can't do that."

Trina touched her cheek so they could see each other's eyes. "Do you love Brendon?"

"With all my heart."

"Then you need to talk to him."

Megan started to protest, but Trina placed a finger against her lips.

"If he sends you away, you will at least have a clear conscience."

"Do you think he will?"

Trina shook her head. "I've adored that man most of my life and feel I know him well. Brendon loves you more than anyone else he's ever loved, including Noelle and me put together. Forgiveness is a powerful thing. Right now, there's nothing that has happened that can't be undone. If I understand him, Brendon went away to clear his mind. My guess is he will return soon."

"You didn't answer me. Will he send me away?"

Trina gave her a sad smile. "That's something the two of you will need to work out." Her new friend grabbed her coat, but stopped at the door. "I'm praying for both of you. But if it goes the wrong way, you know where I live. I've got a shoulder to cry on and a warm bed to sleep in if you need it. God be with you, Megan."

The lights of Trina's departing Mercedes were intersected by those of the Uber driver. Megan glanced at her bags sitting in the kitchen. They sat right in front of the counter where she and Brendon had talked and cooked together so many times.

Megan decided Trina was right. She needed to talk to the man. With that in mind, she tipped the driver and sent him away by himself.

Orville suddenly stood, gazing out into the night. The dog softly woofed, and then stepped from the porch into the yard. In the distance, the sound of an approaching vehicle split the night.

"God, please help me. Help us work this out."

Orville's tail began to wag as the old Ford's headlights lit the porch. It stopped and the night went dark. The interior lamps highlighted Brendon. He seemed to be in a hurry to get out. The man rushed around the hood but suddenly stopped when he noticed her standing there.

"Megan?"

She realized her future would be determined in the next few minutes, but what would happen? Would he accept her apology or were they over?

***

After the unsuccessful search for the park ranger, Brendon took a few moments to ponder the mystery. Slowly, the realization that the man had been an angel took root in his mind. Another strange encounter from his past replayed in his memory. Once when he was little, he'd been playing in the forest by himself. Not paying attention, he'd got himself good and lost.

Night had come fast and Brendon was disoriented, not to mention scared out of his mind. Out of nowhere, a man appeared. He told Brendon he was part of a search party and led Brendon home. But when Brendon turned at the front porch to thank him, the man was nowhere in sight. His parents told him there hadn't been a search party; they thought he was staying with a friend. Brendon now realized the face of the man back then was the same as the ranger's tonight.

Humbled, Brendon bowed his head. "Why would you send an angel to me, Lord, unworthy as I am?"

While there was no audible sound, a feeling grew in his chest. It was as if someone was whispering, "The measure you use to judge others will be the same as I use to judge you."

He understood completely and knew what he needed to do. "Forgive my foolish pride and selfish ways. Help me to understand what she faced and help me forgive Megan. I need to beg for her mercy after the cruel things I said. If there's any way possible, Lord, please don't let it be too late."

He started the faithful Ford and headed home. *Suppose she left with that man?*

A verse from Mark, Chapter 10 filled his heart. *'What God has brought together, let no man separate.'*

Determination flowed from the Eternal Source into his entire being. Even if Megan had returned to London, Brendon would follow her and make her understand how much he loved her. After all, God joined them together. "I will win your heart, Megan, and show you I'm worthy of your love. That I promise you." His foot pressed the accelerator pedal closer to the floor.

The digital numbers on the radio read twelve-fifteen when he threw the shifter into park. Running to the front of the pickup, he stopped when he caught sight of her. *Thank You for keeping her here.*

"Megan?"

"Hi, Brendon. I've been waiting to speak with you."

He touched her hands and found them ice cold. "You're freezing. I need to talk with you, too. Let's go inside where it's warm."

She nodded and he followed her into the cozy kitchen. He noted the luggage stacked against the counter. Did that mean she was planning to leave? *I need to convince her to stay.*

"Let's sit and talk, okay?"

She frowned and opened her mouth, but he spoke first. "I need to beg your forgiveness for the way I treated you."

Dread began to build as he observed her reaction. "Why? I'm the one who should ask for mercy."

"Can we begin by both agreeing to go back to where we were before your friend showed up?"

"Just like that?"

"Yes. You wanted to explain what was happening and I acted the fool. Can you tell me now what you wanted to say?"

With a dazed expression, Megan told him about her childhood, growing up poor. She explained about her grandmother and the will. Anger ran through his veins when she mentioned the clause and what she would need to do to earn her inheritance.

"I think that was the cruelest thing I've ever heard. That money should be yours without requiring you to marry that idiot."

She took his hand with both of hers. "I didn't want the money for me. I wanted to use it to help others."

As she continued, he read between the lines. Megan earned his admiration because she had planned to put others' needs before her own wants.

"What are you going to do? Will you marry him?"

"No. Even if you and I are over, I refuse to be with him."

"But why? You could live life enjoying every luxury possible. Why wouldn't you?"

"Because you've shown me what true love really is. There are greater treasures than the almighty pound, and I've found mine in you. I love you, Brendon."

"I love you, too. I appreciate you sharing what you faced. May I tell you how God sent me back to you tonight?"

"He did what?"

Megan's eyes filled with wonder at his story of the encounter with a ranger who hadn't been real, in an earthly sense.

"I felt a message come into my heart. I understood I was the one who was wrong and I needed to see you and ask for your mercy."

When they'd both finished, they sat there staring at one another.

It was Megan who broke the silence. "Where do we go from here?"

A wild thought entered Brendon's mind. "Hold that thought. I'll be back in a jiffy, as you Brits say."

In less than a minute, he made the round trip to his room and found himself before her. "Do you mind standing?"

"Okay," Megan replied with curiosity as she elevated out of the chair. "Now what?"

"This."

Megan's eyes were as large as dinner plates when Brendon dropped to his knee and opened the box he'd purchased weeks before.

"Megan, will you—"

"Yes, yes, yes!" she screamed as she threw herself at him. Wrapping her arms around his head, Megan kissed him deeply.

When they both paused to draw a breath, Brendon asked, "Does this mean we're engaged—again?"

"Absolutely, but for real this time."

"Do you think anyone will believe us after today?"

"Who cares? God brought us together for a reason—and I've never been happier."

"Me neither," he managed to get out before her lips explored his again. "Our life together can finally begin—without being a lie."

Epilogue

"*A*nd this is where it all happened?" Megan knew Pastor Rollins was teasing them. Once again, Megan and Brendon were hosting desserts on the Hemlock Trail in the equipment building. It was hard to believe a year had passed.

It was Brendon who replied. "We had so much fun the first time around, we thought we'd do it again."

The good pastor shook his head after taking a sip of coffee. "Hopefully you won't come up with something to top last's year's event. I still remember how the two of you stood up in church the Sunday after last year's Hemlock Trail and explained to everyone what happened." He looked directly at Brendon. "Then you described the meeting with the park ranger and the advice he gave. And how when you went back, there were no footprints in the snow. I think it might have been your guardian angel."

"I believe that's true."

"And the powerful message about forgiveness he gave you. I'm certain there wasn't a dry eye in the sanctuary that morning after you two finished."

"I know I was blubbering like a fool when Brendon told that last bit," Megan giggled as she replied. "It was all part of God's plan."

A blur of red and green arrived before them.

"Momma, would you like a cookie? Aunt Trina and I made the oatmeal and M&M ones yesterday just for you."

"Thank you, sweetheart. I think I would." Megan suddenly grasped her stomach. "Whoa! I think your sister might want one as well. She jumped when she heard your voice."

Chloe placed her head against Megan's belly and whispered something to the unborn child within. After offering treats to both Brendon and Pastor Rollins, she spun off to share the goodies with others.

"You two changed that girl's life. Did you see that happy smile?" He again shook his head as he took them in. "You not only adopted her, you brought joy to that little girl's soul. Doing so before Jennifer's passing brought comfort as well. Jennifer was able to die in peace." He suddenly laughed. "It was touching how Chloe just talked to her future sibling."

Megan felt Brendon take her hand and squeeze it. "Love and family are everything to us."

They chatted with the man for a few more moments before he moved on. The lady who had been the maid of honor at their wedding stopped by. There was a glow on Trina's face as she held hands with the man she would soon marry.

"The event is going well, don't you think?"

"I believe Jim and I can take some of the credit for that," Brendon joked as he playfully smacked Trina's boyfriend's shoulder. "We spent all day yesterday in the freezing cold decorating the place, while you ladies relaxed in the warmth inside."

"And baked one hundred dozen cookies and eighty pies," Trina replied with a false expression of irritation. "I noted both of you had the special cookies Chloe and I made just for you. Did you enjoy them?" Both Brendon and Megan nodded. "Good, we also made..." Trina's voice trailed off and her eyes focused on something behind them.

The married couple turned, observing Taylor walking toward them. Brendon's sister's lips were pursed together as she led a man in their direction.

"Do you know who that is?" Brendon whispered to his wife.

"Unfortunately, I do. Remember the jerk from last year's party?"

"Your other fiancé?" Brendon snickered after he delivered the one-liner.

"I'll ignore that. Anyway, this is his grandfather."

Taylor and the man arrived. Taylor spoke next. "Here's another man claiming to be George Chamberlain. He was asking for you, Megan."

"Thank you, Taylor." Megan took the man's hand when he offered it.

"You look radiant, Megan. You resemble your grandmother when she was a young lady." He glanced at Megan's protruding stomach and smiled. "It seems marriage agrees with you."

"It does. How may I help you?"

"Is this your husband?" George asked as he nodded in Brendon's direction.

"That I am."

Megan picked up on the shift in Brendon's tone. Her husband took a step so he was between Megan and the older man.

"My wife asked what you wanted."

The gentleman's laughter seemed out of place for the situation. "I, sir, am here to right a wrong."

"Excuse me?" Megan was confused by his words.

"My namesake and grandson, well, he was your grandmother's lawyer. He probated her will."

"I remember."

"I was shocked to learn of the 'requirements' your grandmother made in her will. Of all the years I'd known her, she never once suggested she would do something that drastic. But then, I know how much she despised America and its citizens."

His words were bringing up bad memories. "Thanks for the history lesson. Why are you here?"

"My, how your impatience also reminds me of your grandmother, God rest her soul."

"Again, my wife asked you a question." The tone of Brendon's voice was a little sharper.

"Let me answer. My grandson was involved in a nasty accident last spring. Almost lost his life. That moment changed him. He turned to God and is working hard to live a good life."

"Good for him," Megan added flatly. "How is this pertinent?"

"Because," the man said with a large smile, "his new conscience wouldn't rest until he righted his wrong."

"What do you mean?"

"He confessed to me how he changed your grandmother's will after her death. He was the one who added the requirements for you to marry him and live in London so you could receive your inheritance."

Megan's face heated. Anger filled her mind. "He did what?"

"He cheated you, Megan. That was the bad part. I'd like you to know he has since self-reported his actions. He will no longer practice law and is facing the legal ramifications of stealing your inheritance. He will be imprisoned, but the man has given his life to Jesus. There is also a good part—for you."

"Let me see if I heard you correctly. He took what was rightfully mine and now, because of his conscience, came clean. He did all that so he could sleep at night. But I'm still the one who was rooked."

"You *were*, as in the past tense." George the second reached into his pocket and extracted an envelope, which he offered to Megan. "Here is a cashier's check for the full amount of your inheritance, with interest."

Megan felt light-headed and reached for Brendon. Her husband's arm steadied her.

"I'm not sure I heard you right."

"You did. My apologies for everything you went through. Here is everything that your grandmother willed to you. Merry Christmas, Megan, and enjoy your future. Your happiness is all she really ever wanted."

With those words, George Chamberlain spun on his heels and departed. Megan was shaking all over. Somehow, she opened the envelope and her mouth fell open.

"I've never seen this much money," she whispered to Brendon. "Have you?"

"Nope. Well, it looks like you can have anything in the world you want."

She spun and faced the man whose last name she shared. "I have everything I need, because I have you. Figures on a ledger or gold in a safe can't buy what God has given me."

"And what's that?"

She waved her hand to everything around her. "Family, friends, an eternal future and the love of the one man God made for me."

"But with that check, you're extremely wealthy now."

"I was already rich before today. My treasures are stored in Heaven and guaranteed by God's word. Sure, we'll be able to help others with what we've been given today, but this money couldn't buy what I cherish the most."

"And that is?"

"A clear conscience, love of family, dear friends, salvation when I'm gone and the eternal love you and I share." Megan kissed him. "Let's go celebrate the real meaning of the season—the greatest gift ever given—Jesus."

Brendon touched Megan's belly and whispered to the child within, "You're lucky, kiddo. You're gonna have the best mom in the world."

With his words, the baby moved. A different sensation accompanied the child's movement.

"Brendon?"

"Yes?"

"I think we did it."

"What are you talking about?"

"Topping last year's Hemlock Trail."

"What do you mean?"

"I'm afraid my water just broke. The baby's coming."

Brendon held her. "And just like her mother, our little girl will be the center of attention. We better not host the event next year. Know why?"

Pain rolled across her stomach. "Why's that?"

"We'd have to have twins."

***

Brendon brushed some loose strands of hair from Megan's face. He held a sleeping Chloe on his lap.

"You look beautiful, sweetheart."

Megan glanced at the bundle of warmth swaddled in a blanket in her arms. She couldn't help but smile.

"I think we should name her either Joy or Merry."

"I like those names, but I'd also like to suggest we consider Bliss or Cherie."

"Nice ones. Wait, I came across the name Amara the other day."

"That's pretty. What does it mean?"

"It means the everlasting love God gives us never fails."

While holding Chloe, Brendon leaned in to kiss his new daughter and then his wife.

"We are rich, aren't we?"

"In the important things. I love you, Brendon."

"I love you, Megan. I'm so glad God made you for me."

Their lips met again as the four of them snuggled against each other, thanking God for His blessings... and dreaming of eternity, together.

If you liked *A Catoctin Christmas*, you'll love these...

Destiny

Selena is at a crossroads in life. Trey has everything, except someone to love. This once happy couple went their separate ways years ago. But when they cross paths again, each wonders, were they meant to be each other's destiny?

Scan this QR code to order *Destiny*, a *South Mountain Journey of Faith* second chance novel.

Paperback   *Large Print*

The Lonely Road

Elise is still adjusting to real life, but wishes she could find a close friend. Landon moved to a new area to fulfill his dreams, yet yearns for someone who will share it with him. Both feel an emptiness inside. Could it be they are the answer to each other's dreams?

Promises

Emily's life didn't turn out as planned. Instead of curing diseases and enjoying a life of travel, she's rooted to her parents' orchard. Tyler never fulfilled the promise he made to Emily years ago. At their daughters' softball game, they meet again. Is it too late to make good on an old promise?

Paperback   *Large Print*

Backroads

All Julia ever wanted was a man who would love her more than anything. When she meets Grant, Julia thinks she's met Mr. Right. But when he leaves for a long-term work assignment, it appears Grant's job is more important. Will God ever answer her prayers?

Dreams

Abbigail is ashamed of the sultry life she's lived. She desperately wants to change her ways.

Jenson is a man at the top of his world, until a short vacation to Italy awakens a new dream.

They are brought together to decide what's best for an elderly man, Jenson's estranged father. At first, they go together like olive oil and sparkling water. But is the reason for them coming together simply to make a decision about the old man, or did God unite them to help each other fulfill their dreams?

Paperback

Large Print

Jubilee

Madison lost everything and is living in her car. She seeks out Eleanor, the sister she said was as good as dead to her. Will Eleanor help Madison?

God brings a caring young man and his mother into Madison's life. The woman accepts Madison as the daughter she never had. Then, during what should be the happiest day in Madison's life, the mistake that brought her downfall confronts her in person. Even with her sister and her future mother-in-law by her side, can Madison overcome her demons and conquer her past?

Want to read more of Chas's books?

*Get **Skating in Paradise** free when you subscribe to the newsletter.*

Visit www.ChasWilliamson.com *to claim your free book!*

Every day is a struggle for oncology nurse Tammy Kunkle. After cancer took both her little girl and husband, she's dedicated her life solely to helping others. But when she visits a former child patient, she's introduced to a man filled with a warm, faithful spirit. Could it be Tammy has met her new future?

Download your free copy of *Skating in Paradise* today.

www.chaswilliamson.com

Did you like
A Catoctin Christmas?
Please consider leaving a review for other readers.

For a complete list of
Chas's books visit
www.ChasWilliamson.com

Dedication

We've been together so long, it's all but impossible to remember a time we weren't us. And just like Megan and Brendon, we overcame a seemingly endless string of challenges—the challenge of careers, shift work, children, college, and the list goes on and on. Together, we journeyed through the fuzzy beginning years, raising kids, the empty nest and retirement. Now we find ourselves in our golden years. I never dreamed my life would be this blessed—and it is because of you. The memories we've built—from "Ugh, teeth" to that first kiss as man and wife to renewing our vows on the sands of Oahu—you have made my life a fairy tale. And when I look back, I would do it all over again (except maybe next time I'd book that night at the Old Faithful Lodge). ☺

I've lived a life of adventure and our life together has been the greatest one. And because of God's promises, I know we will be together for all eternity.

You are the greatest blessing of my life and I love you more than mere words could ever state and I dedicate *A Catoctin Christmas* to you.

Our once-in-a-lifetime story can be summed up in one sentence—"And they lived happily-ever-after."

I love you forever!

Acknowledgments

To God, for showering me with so many blessings.

To Jesus, for making the sacrifice to cleanse our sins and the Holy Spirit for life-changing inspiration.

To Janet, my soulmate. They said we'd never make it, but we did. And our story is more than making it. We've created the greatest love story I've ever heard.

To my children. My wish for you is that God blesses you as he has Mom and me.

To our grandchildren... thank you for the memories and good times. Proverbs 17:6 says, "Grandchildren are the crown of the aged." The three of you are the gems in the crowns Mimi and I now wear. Always remember how much we love you.

To Demi, editor, publisher and friend. Did you think that after getting the messy draft of the first book that we'd reach book twenty-five? Hopefully you are proud of how I applied everything you taught me. Thank you!

To the beta-reading team of Janet, Sarah, Mary, Bekah and Diane and your guidance as we traveled to *Catoctin*.

To all who feel life passed them by—know this. If you can dream it, you have the power to make it come true.

To my fans. May God bless and inspire you through my meager words—ones He placed in my heart. Thank you for being a fan!

About the Author

Chas Williamson's lifelong dream was to write. He started writing his first book at age eight, but quit after two paragraphs. Yet some dreams never fade...

It's said one should write what one knows best. That left two choices—the world of environmental health and safety... or romance. Chas and his bride have built a fairytale life of love. At her encouragement, he began writing romance. The characters you'll meet in his books are very real to him, and he hopes they'll become just as real to you.

True Love Lasts Forever!

Follow Chas on www.bookbub.com

 Check out our website at ChasWilliamson.com

 Check us out on Facebook at Chas Williamson Books

 Follow us on Instagram at Chas Williamson